SOUTH AUSTIN VAMPIRE

A BLUE-EYED INDIAN MYSTERY

SOUTH AUSTIN VAMPIRE

RUSS HALL

FIVE STAR
A part of Gale, Cengage Learning

GALE
CENGAGE Learning™

Detroit • New York • San Francisco • New Haven, Conn • Waterville, Maine • London

LIBRARY OF CONGRESS CATALOGING-IN-PUBLICATION DATA

Hall, Russ, 1949–
    South Austin vampire : a blue-eyed Indian mystery / Russ Hall.
  — 1st ed.
    p. cm.
    ISBN-13: 978-1-59414-866-8 (hardcover)
    ISBN-10: 1-59414-866-X (hardcover)
    1. Private investigators—Fiction. 2. Murder—Investigation—
Fiction. 3. Austin (Tex.)—Fiction. I. Title.
PS3558.A37395S68 2010
813'.54—dc22   2010024853

Published in 2010 in conjunction with Tekno Books and Ed Gorman.

Printed in Mexico
2 3 4 5 6 7 14 13 12 11

Now laughing friends deride
Tears I cannot hide.
So I smile and say,
When a lovely flame dies,
Smoke gets in your eyes.

—Otto Harbach

CHAPTER ONE

You go out on a late spring Austin night—when a surprise heat wave has settled in and even after midnight it's so sticky and hot the street dogs are trying to rub off their fur—and you're liable to find anything, from the future love of your life and someday potential ex-spouse, to a dead body on the corner.

A small crowd had formed even though the light was not good. The first cruiser to arrive pulled up and the officers climbed out and pushed their way through the curious until they could see the body.

"Damn, she's sure white for a Latino," the patrolman said, while the sergeant called it in. If this were South Congress that would mean hooker. The clothes looked wrong. Maybe a student or housewife.

The sergeant moved the people back while the patrolman poked until he found a small purse he handed up to the sergeant. "Why's she so damned pale?"

The sound of a distant siren weaving its way through traffic, with occasional blasts of its horn, now headed their way.

With one finger the patrolman moved her head to the other side. His head jerked back an inch and his eyes widened. On the side of her parchment white neck he could see two holes, a touch of red in each, about the distance apart a set of human canines would make if they were long. Real long. "Oh please, God, tell me this isn't what I think it is."

The sergeant moved the small knot of people further back.

He shook his head. The shit was going to hit the fan no matter what. He looked down the street, could see the flashing lights as the siren got louder.

Not so far away, I drove a car I didn't care for through a town I would find I didn't know as well as I thought I did, but whatever was going to hit the fan was nevertheless going to hit me too.

I first ran into Lola Pillaccherosi that same black night in the parking lot behind the Devil's Due, an Austin live music spot tucked away in a dark stretch of Third Street. The club, with its dark brick and wrought iron facade, red neon sign topped by two horns, had, for quite a while, been in the slow evolutionary process of becoming a folk and blues music venue after a short stint as a grunge band dive. I got out of my car to see what damage had been done to my fender.

This happened in late March, on one of those Texas spring nights where the sky had been clear and robin egg blue all day, but now had shifted to a starless solid black except for a razor-edge sickle of a moon, the kind so full of omen and portent even the black cats pause to look up before crossing their own paths. I half expected to hear the howl of a wolf or at least a coyote in the distance, but got only the usual downtown city noises at this hour: impatient horns, a low squeal of tires, and the muffled music coming from inside the club—sounded like the haunting strains of that old blues classic "St. James Infirmary" from where I stood. The temperature by day had been in the eighties, but it had dropped all the way into the high seventies and seemed to want to do something—rain or just be clammy. In spite of the heat I felt a chill and turned up the collar of my suit jacket.

I had been due at the club hours earlier. A pile of missing persons' cases had me dashing to a lot of places I'd have otherwise avoided. I'd gotten tied up at the police forensics lab watching Vito Obregón slice open a floater so ripe the corpse had come apart like a piñata. It's something I would have preferred to skip, but I *had* been the one to find the body. I still had dabs of Vicks up my nose against that smell, and the damp air around me seemed to carry the faint odor of eucalyptus.

The thought of heading home and coming back another time crossed my thoughts just before the grating clash of fender and bumper eliminated all other options, not that there was anything to go home to except an empty office, a third of a bottle of hundred-percent blue agave tequila, and a cot that missed Cassie as much as I did. That's why I had kept my tired feet moving.

I was easing along, looking for an open parking space when Lola backed out in an abrupt whirl of flying gravel with no lights on. My battered Timex that had taken many a licking said 1:20 A.M. Breathy saxophone notes that only I hear squeezed up and down discordant scales in some far corner of my skull. The notes came to an abrupt halt with that clang of fender metal.

Her door swung open and she reeled out of the driver's side, went to stand up and nearly did a forward cartwheel. She grabbed at the top of the door and pulled herself upright, slapped at the door when it moved back and forth beneath her grip.

"Just where in purple-balled hell did you think you were going?" she yelled.

A guy with her got out of the passenger seat, more slowly than she had erupted. He looked across the top of her car, as if getting a good look at her for the first time. His face twisted into the knot of someone biting into a sour, perhaps rotten, lemon—her looks were fine, even stunning, but she had an edge to her attitude that would make a pit bull nervous. His head swung to me and he seemed as little impressed as anyone can get about a member of the same species.

She started into a tirade, and it made a fireworks show of some language I hadn't heard before or since the locker room. If there had been any sailors near, they'd have crept away, embarrassed. I stood by the open door of my car, waiting for her to wind down. Against the buildings across from me I saw reflections of the swirls of blue and red lights approaching. For once, I welcomed seeing them.

The cruiser pulled up, but that didn't slow her down. She still turned the air as blue as some of the police car's lights when two patrolmen crunched across the gravel toward us. Their right hands rested on the butts of their guns, but they hadn't drawn them, or even loosened the safety straps. One of them talked into a small square black microphone fastened to his collarbone, calling for a backup car I guessed.

The uniform closest to me tried to get a word in, finally slid a few steps closer to me, and said from the side of his mouth, "She hit you?"

"She was backing without lights. I didn't see her."

Lola heard just enough between her own ranting to spin on us. She had medium long hair, dark hair that held a reddish sheen even in the dim light of the parking lot. Her eyes were very big and brown, full of sparks.

"Didn't see me," she roared. "I thought you Injun types were supposed to be so damned good at seeing in the dark." I had to give her this: I do have a face, high cheekbones and all, that— except for my blue eyes—looks like I ought to be out in front of a tobacco store with a fistful of cigars and wearing a wooden smile. Then again, I'm not unknown in Austin's music biz circles. Neither were good excuses, though, for her to pick on my heritage.

The cop near me reached for my extended driver's license

and PI ticket. The other one edged closer to the woman. Neither of them saw the guy who'd been with her ease through the cars in the lot and slip away in the dark. I envied him.

Another police car pulled in behind the one already parked. Both had kept their lights going. I knew a little about the law, and if this woman would calm down and keep her mouth clamped she could probably get off with just a scolding. We were still on private property and she hadn't been driving outside the lot. She *was* carrying a load and would have been tagged for DWI, and tagged hard, if she had gotten onto the street, had to know she sailed well within range of a public intoxication rap. Both police cars had been close, too close, in patrolling the area.

"So you're a private dick, huh?" the cop near me said. "What're you doing here? On a case?" His eyes scanned me and took in my suit, the tie, the fact that my shirt collar was buttoned at this hour.

"Had an appointment with the club's owner, Owen Peasey. Why?"

"You know her?" He nodded to the shouting woman as he handed my cards back.

"Don't know her from Adam's house cat." I could see from the dark long coat that flapped open as she gestured that she wore some sort of costume, the kind you'd don if you were appearing in lights before a crowd—something shiny and red, with a slit that went all the way up one side of a tanned and taut leg.

"How can I be close to resisting arrest," she shouted, "if you can't arrest me for anything? He's the one who hit *my* car."

The cop who'd been talking to me walked over that way, and I followed. He was what I might call beefy if asked to say anything polite on that topic. The rectangular brass plate on his uniform said Newman. He had three stripes on his shoulder.

Lola talked, at least in a lower tone, to the other three cops.

She spun when she felt Sergeant Newman approach. The first words out of her mouth were, "You know, a man your size shouldn't wear blue. You stand on a corner and open your mouth and people are liable to start shoving mail in."

I held back a smile. It was sure not the right thing to say to Sergeant Newman, whose politeness so far he'd managed by repression, not native good will.

"Make her walk the line," he said. "Unless she'd rather go the Breathalyzer route."

If those dark eyes of hers had thrown sparks before, they turned into volcanoes now. For the first time her mouth stayed closed—that is, until she had to do the alphabet drill.

I heard one of the cops say her name out loud, with a touch of recognition. Austin's claim as the Live Music Capital of America made meeting a star like Lola under these circumstances surprise me less than it might have. He didn't say anything like that about me, though the local paper insisted on referring to me as "the Blue-Eyed Indian," and had more than once also referred to me as the detective to Austin's music stars after a couple of recent cases.

Tell you the truth, I could stay home and listen to the drainpipe moanings and the world would probably churn along fine without me. All of us, though, have the tiny threads that tie us to the rest of the planet and people on it, and the work you do is often that. Each of us has particular skills and feels needed because of them or we'd be over the edge of the cliff *en masse,* like a herd of rabid lemmings.

I didn't have anything like Lola's degree of fame and none of her looks and star quality. I had noticed that Lola's face, when in repose, looked more than just attractive. It struck me as memorable. She weathered the DWI drill, tottered along the line, and did okay until she had to stand still at the end. Then she almost did a nosedive.

"Miss Pillaccherosi," Sergeant Newman finally said. "We're not going to press any charges. We'll just write up the accident for your insurance companies." When she started to speak, he held up a finger. "But you're in no condition to drive. Is there anyone here who can see that you get home?"

She looked at her car for the first time in a while, saw that the passenger had scooted long ago. A flash of color ran across her face. Her head turned back slowly. She looked at me. "Him," she said. "He's going to drive me home."

Sergeant Newman gave me a look while she backed her car into its space, got her purse, and locked up her car. I shrugged, never said a word. She climbed into my car, gave me her address, and sat quiet for the first twenty blocks. Most of the traffic lights at this hour had been switched over to flashing red, so I stopped and started a lot on the way to her place.

"A Volvo," she said at last. "I'd have never figured you for a Volvo man."

"It was a gift."

She turned sideways to look at me. "You don't look like the kind of person people give gifts to." The glance I caught registered her frown. I don't know why some guys are drawn to women who never smile, but enough of them had been attracted to Lola. Her past was paved with a cobblestone path of broken hearts, if half the stories about her could be believed.

There were circumstances. I didn't want to go into all that— the money that came up missing in that investigation, or the cop, Borster, who still thought I had it. Up close, she had smooth youthful skin and a wide, sensual mouth. She filled the car with a smell that might have been part jasmine, part sandalwood. While the cops were putting her through the paces I had gotten the Vicks out of my nose. Her scent was almost worth the drive.

"You didn't have to drive me home, you know," she said. I

turned onto her street. "I can be kind of a bitch sometimes."

I left that alone. "Who was the guy who skipped out on you?" I asked.

She let out a small puff of air through her nose and looked out her window. "Just some guy I thought I knew."

Another block down, she said, "I don't particularly like Volvos, or the people who drive them."

"Me neither," I said. "But I try not to dwell on it."

I had to slow and watch the numbers until I came to her place. We were in a pretty classy part of town. Each lot sprawled across a couple of acres. The homes all started in the three-quarters of a million range, and some moved steeply upward in price. She gave me no help with the directions. I turned into her drive. The headlights swung across a very smooth and perfect green lawn.

"I had the damn thing cemented over and covered with artificial turf," she said. "My ex liked to mow. I don't. The neighbors hate me now. But at least it's not sucking a gallon of water per square foot each day like their damned Saint Augustine or even the ones with Bermuda grass."

Her place—a three-story modern brick near-mansion that seemed to cry out that you would find neither two-point-five children nor a dog on the grounds—seemed like a lot of house in which to live in alone.

When I stopped, she swung to me, waited. I kept my hands on the wheel, turned my head. "What?"

"Nothing," she said, and got out. I waited until she was inside, then drove to my place.

The phone was ringing as I wrestled with the lock of my small office on Brazos Street at a little after 3 A.M. I sleep on a cot in the tiny back room. In my misguided mood of the moment, I thought it might be Lola calling to share a more sincere thanks.

14

Instead it was a harsh voice, like rusty nails being ripped from plywood.

"When you least expect it, expect it." The phone clicked dead.

That was Detective Sergeant Borster. Since my last case he would drive by my place at least two or three times a week, not stopping or saying anything, just giving me the beady eye. Then, there were these calls.

Some time back I had been on a case where he missed out on a huge reward, for which he blamed me. The next time our paths collided, some laundered munitions money came up missing. Borster had saved me a lot of awkwardness with an overzealous, reputation-seeking FBI Special Agent, but I found out later it was because he thought I had the loot. A quick check of my finances and a look at my lifestyle should have set him straight. I did get a new suit and car (albeit one I wouldn't have picked out myself) for wrapping up that case—both sent him false signals. Borster had carved his reputation as a police detective not with a rocket scientist's mind, but with the bulldog stubbornness of the late General Grant.

I felt too filleted and tired to do more than hang up my rumpled suit and crawl onto the cot. As Scarlett O'Hara once put it, tomorrow was indeed another day.

What with all the work I needed to do on that missing persons' case, a couple of nights peeled by before I got around to calling on Owen Peasey as I'd promised him I would. The club seemed to be hopping, hitting its midnight stride as I wedged inside. A young black singer with promise gripped the mike and swayed in the beam from a baby klieg while pouring out his soul. His sax player, though, stole the show while trying hard not to. I joined a row of patrons crammed shoulder to shoulder at the bar, finally saw Owen a half hour later bending over a table during the break between sets. He spotted me and hustled over, pushing his way through people with the seasoned flair of someone who had carried trays through thicker herds than this.

"Trav," he called out. "Where the hell you been?"

"Just knocking around," I said.

"Jeez Louise. I thought you were coming a couple of nights ago."

Some of Owen's close and personal friends called him "Jeezy" Peasey. I still called him Owen. He was a round but muscular short fellow, with stiff bristly black hair wherever it was normal to have hair, except the top of his head. He'd been a singer wannabe in his own youth, but had neither the looks nor quite enough talent. The ability bar had been raised very high in Austin, which is why you find some extremely skilled people working in dives.

"Jimmy Bravuro told me about that woman helping you with something, one a your cases. Jeez, is she a terror, or what? Did any of those backwoods militia she didn't pop ever go after her?"

"Yeah," I said, "and the one I know about came back with more stitches than a baseball." He spoke of Joz Brosche, and just the thought of her made an ice cube crawl sideways up my spine. She's the one who had ended up with the money Borster craved. The only good thing to come of that mess had been meeting Cassie, and now she had drifted out of the picture too, though I hardly thought about that at all, except once or twice every half-dozen moments. "Tell me what's on your mind. Your problem didn't go away on its own, did it?"

"No. Afraid not."

The people at the bar around us crowded close. "Can you tell me more about . . . ?" I started to ask. He held up the palm of one stubby hand at me.

"That'll have to come from her." He nodded to the stage.

16

The lights in the club dimmed.

Lola stepped out onto the stage, in a blue dress this time, much on the model of the red one I'd seen. This dress shimmered and flowed with her as she moved. The baby spot picked up on her stroll to the mike at the center of the stage and stayed with her. Wisps of smoke from the audience lifted and swirled in the beam of light. Clubs weren't supposed to allow smoking, but at this hour Owen let people light up until a fire marshal said otherwise.

She sang, and I mean she could *sing*. Her eyes pressed shut. She leaned close to the mike and her hips swayed ever so slightly. From somewhere deep inside herself she tapped raw emotion. It had to hurt to sing like that, had to be physically draining. When she sang of losing someone, you knew she *had* lost someone. She had the kind of range and passion that makes goose bump chills and warm flushes rush through you as you listen. I glanced around. It wasn't just me. The room had gotten stone quiet except for her and the small backup combo. Every face transfixed on her. All talking stopped.

Lights that swept across her and kept her in the focus at the center of the stage shifted in tints. First her dress looked green, then lavender. The moods that shifted across her face to match the songs seemed as chameleon.

She sang a wide range of tunes, including "You Can Have My Husband, But Please Don't Mess With My Man." She shifted to a couple of request tunes from a man in a suit who sat alone at a small table near the stage. For him she went back in time to sing "String of Pearls," and "Smoke Gets in Your Eyes."

She made me aware of what people mean when they say larger than life. I could sense every man in the room, myself included, falling in love with her for those moments when her voice resonated to the corners of the packed club. Her eyes had a way of sweeping through the crowd and let every individual know she sang just for *you*. The guy at one table shifted in his seat, but kept his eyes locked on her.

When she stopped, there was a moment of shocked quiet, then clapping erupted before people stirred and the place got back to a hum of voices and people called for fresh drinks.

Owen led me backstage, tapped on the door, and shoved me in when he got the "Come in."

She sat in front of a mirror with a string of lights around it. She turned and saw me close the door behind myself.

"Mr. Bad Penny," she said. Her lip curled. "I guess I never got your name. What do you want?"

"Peasey told me you wanted to see me."

"He was wrong. I never said that." She dabbed at the makeup, taking it off. It looked pretty thick—had to be for the lights. A clothes rack that ran along the wall had the usual change of costumes and a lavender feather boa draped over the end. Otherwise the room had bare walls and worn furniture, nothing personal to make it hers. Owen had told me she'd been singing for him since he took over the club and started the shift to become a blues and folk haven.

"Maybe he said you *should* see me," I said. "Any reason for him to think that?"

Where she rubbed the makeup off a bruise showed on her face below her right eye. A row of small bruises ran along the inside of her upper arm, the kind of bruises fingers make.

She watched my face in the mirror, started putting on fresh makeup as soon as she finished taking off the pancake. Her eyes narrowed when they locked with mine. "I think you'd better go."

I thought how different meeting her like this was from seeing her on the stage. People fall for stars all the time, which is why there are fan clubs. Hearing and seeing her on stage, I could understand the crushes. Up close, she could put out the flames with the best of them.

Someone rapped on the door. It swung open before she could say anything, though she had turned at the waist to look that way. A face and shoulders stuck through the partially open door. The man in the suit who sat by himself looked at me, then her. "Oh," he said. "You're busy."

He ducked back out, and the door closed.

I said, "That was?"

"Just some fan."

"You never said who that fellow was with you the night I drove you home."

"That was no fella. That was my husband," she said. She threw a cotton ball toward the wastebasket, made the shot, didn't seem to get much satisfaction from doing that. "My ex-husband." Her lip twisted. "As if I even need to tell you that. Who the hell do you think . . . ? Oh, never mind. Just get the hell out."

"I'm gone," I said. Bruises and all, she looked very attractive, even when angry. But then, I'd never seen her otherwise.

Out in the hallway I looked for Owen. I didn't see him anywhere around. The fellow in the suit stood at the end of the hall at the pay phone. He had his back to me, talking low to someone. I noticed he had one finger depressing the phone's receiver button.

Something felt more than a little off-center. I found Owen in the far packed corner of the bar. A folk singer, Up-And-Down Jonesy, held the stage and sang as if his supper depended on it. His real first name was Darrell, but the locals called him Up-And-Down because he'd been right on the cusp of making it once. His first CD had rocketed, and his second had maintained the promise. Then the sparkle that made him stand out had just left. Some said drink had done it, others said a woman. The tale spun into one of those chicken versus egg stories you hear too often. He could still draw a crowd, but his performance paled after Lola's intensity. His voice did fill the room though, making it hard to talk. I waved Owen outside.

We stepped into the cool evening air. "What do *you* think is up with Lola?" I asked. Stars and the slab of a half-moon hung over us in the black sky.

"Jeez. I got no idea," he said. "That's why I called you. You're the detective. But if she shares anything it's got to come from her. Maybe you can soften her up."

I shook my head. I'd met people who could be softened up. Lola didn't strike me as one of them. Not with words, or even with a bat.

"Give it a little time," Owen suggested. "Maybe poke around on the side, see what you come up with."

I didn't crave yet another case on my plate. In the feast-or-famine business that I did, I was currently feasting, at least in respect to the amount of work I had. A missing well-off person is hard enough to trace. You take several missing people on the opposite end of the social spectrum and you're talking needle in a haystack, big-time. I'd been up and going since early morning and had barely snatched a bite on the run. If I had toothpicks I would have used them to prop open my eyes. If it had been anyone but Owen, I'd have given the whole thing a miss. But Owen had given Jimmy Bravuro and a few others I knew a break now and then, and he'd helped me get a grip on some of the Austin music scene when I was new to town. He'd always shot straight with me, and he wasn't the type to ask for help unless he was really up against it.

I hesitated, then nodded. "Sure. Anyone who could mesmerize a crowd with a voice like hers deserves a little flexing. I'll see what I can find first." I didn't welcome another round with that mouth of hers when it wasn't singing.

The gravel crunched under my feet as I walked out to my car, with its fresh ding on the left front fender. I debated going back in. I needed to know more than I did if I was going to be any help to Owen. Thoughts of the old cot pulled me toward the waiting car. Maybe I should have stayed and taken another try at getting through to her. I probably would have if I'd known that it was the last time I would see her alive.

The stone floor was cold on her bare feet. The draft that swept through the room, making the flames flicker on the rows of candles, shot up from the unforgiving cold of the floor, into the loose black silk robe she wore and across goose bumps on her naked flesh.

Shrieks of pagan music built to a crescendo as she lowered to her knees at the stained altar. A chorus of wails from the others in the room followed the music. She kept her eyes down, could only see the hands that lowered the silver chalice onto the altar in front of her.

She gulped, and reached for the chalice, trying to close her eyes only to have them snap open and stare at the blood. She raised it toward her lips. Just as the rim touched her trembling lower lip, her fingers opened and the silver cup dropped to the floor and spilled. The chorus of wailing stopped. Only the music sounded around the clatter of the chalice. The pool of blood spread until the wet touched her knees. She looked up. It felt like looking at herself in a mirror.

"I want out."

"Are you sure?" The deep masculine voice came from behind her.

"Never more so. Don't tell me it can't be done, either."

"Oh, Lola. No, it's not hard. Getting out is the easiest thing of all."

CHAPTER TWO

Somewhere on or about the clap of doom the next morning, my phone began to ring and would not let up. I staggered from the cot in the back room out to the office. Rain hammered down outside, had been going at it all night. The steady hiss of water running down the front glass accompanied my steps. I'd been dreaming about Borster and expected to hear his raspy drawl when I lifted the receiver.

"Trav?"

"Yeah?"

"Better get over here." Vito sounded rattled. When a medical examiner sounds rattled it's time to step lively. "And oh," he said, "on your way over, stick your head in at St. David's and see if you can cast an eye on that Jose Doe they have there."

"The one in the news?"

"None other."

I put the receiver back on its cradle and the phone rang as soon as I did. It all sounded like one continuous ring in my head.

"What?" I snapped into it.

"Travis?" Much more melodious than Borster, and female.

"Yeah?"

It was Sister Consuela on the other end. I glanced at my watch: 6:30 A.M. "Can you come over here?"

"Give me a chance to shake loose the cobwebs and I'll stop by." I didn't share with her that I had a stop or two to make first. I eased the receiver back onto its cradle and started the tiptoe back to my cot when it rang again.

I turned, sighed, frowned at the half-empty bottle of cactus juice perched on the desk. I went back and picked up the receiver slowly. "Yeah, what is it?" I had half a dozen cases going at once. Hard to tell which of them wanted to rattle my chain next, and at this hour.

"You going to be in the area all day?" It was Cassie.

"Sure. Why? Do I get to smoke 'em if I got 'em?" My heart shot to the top of my chest and started hammering like the late Gene Krupa showing off.

"I'm bringing a prisoner in to town, thought we might squeeze in lunch."

"Sure thing," I said. "I'll just get out my day planner and pencil you in for a power lunch." She would know that the chances of my having a day planner were right up there with Genghis Khan having a favorite charity.

Until Cassie's path crossed mine, in a previous case, I'd always been the guy who my friend Jimmy Bravuro says never gets the girl. That all changed, with head-spinning speed. Why anyone who looked like the prime pick of a Swedish bikini team would have anything to do with a bit of worn shoe leather like me amazed and confounded my friends. Well, it did me too. But life has a way of correcting these temporary wrinkles and she had headed back out to Texas Hill Country to do her job as a peace officer, while I had stayed in Austin, occasionally upping the doses of tequila I take to prevent the snake bite. In fairness, I've not had the snake bite. She had become a memory, a pleasant enough one, with just enough lingering presence for the guys to kid me that I might have a thing for women in uniforms. Oh, I didn't think about Cassie too much. That's why lightning bolts of electricity shot up and down my limbs as I held the phone.

When I hung up I did feel awake enough to head for the shower, knowing it would be lukewarm at best and have a faint rust color and smell to it. But there was almost a hop to my step. Borster, in what usually passes for charm with him, had asked me, "What I want to know is how something like that ever got interested in you. You part-Indians aren't hung like Ronnie Salami too, are you?" Always sensitive. That was Borster.

The problem with that, I thought as I scraped the sponge across the tired frame, is that when you live as alone as I do, sometimes you even start numbering people like Borster among your friends. All that had changed a hue when Cassie came on the scene, changed again when she left. She lived an hour-and-a-half from town, but got in once every blue moon or so. The ray of hope swelled me like a sailboat's spinnaker in a Force Five wind. It was almost enough to remind me I was human.

I arrived ahead of visiting hours at the hospital and slipped in past a guard—not even a speed bump for me, a good thing given the busy slate I had for the day—and headed for the ICU where the Hispanic coma victim lay. I clicked along the hard tiles of the hallway, my damp suit leaving behind a drop here and there. No one stopped me. I felt and looked like a man on a mission.

The Jose Doe, as Vito had put it, had been found on the street in a coma. The newspapers and electronic media had been giving him a fair amount of ink and air time. This seemed the kind of mystery they craved and could sink their teeth into. So far, no one had come forward to claim Jose, though his face had been getting fairly well known.

I'd been to this intensive care unit a time or two before, most recently to watch a fifteen-year-old gangbanger breathe his last after being gut-shot and spending most of the night huddled by trash cans in an alley. His folks told me they thought he had been with a church group the night he got shot. They'd stood shoulder-to-shoulder beside me, looking through the glass as the boy died.

Jose Doe lay in a center bed of a three-bed room, the white sheets pulled up to his chin. The tanned look of his face contrasted with the white hospital starkness. Someone had combed his hair and seen that he got shaved. Tubes ran from his nose. He hadn't come to, nor did it seem likely to me that he would.

I turned and saw a woman with a pail and mop looking at me. She wore green hospital scrubs. Her hair had been tucked into a net. She wore about four hundred years of world weariness sketched in the lines of her dark face. I saw something else there too. Hope maybe.

I went over to the nurses' station. "Ginny," I said.

A tall, redheaded nurse who had a few years on me spun from a computer screen. She carried the obligatory clipboard in one hand. "What are you doing roaming around in here? You on another case?" She winked, but came over and put an arm in mine, firmly leading me out.

"That cleaning woman back there," I said in a lowered voice. "She been with you long?"

Ginny glanced back. "A week or two. Why? Help's hell to come by these days. I hope you don't have anything on her."

"Just curious," I said.

Ginny eased me through the exit door and closed it behind me.

"What's the deal with Jose Doe?" I said to Vito Obregón when he opened the door and let me drip into the Forensic Department's morgue. He held out a jar of Vicks and I started unscrewing the lid.

"He's not one of the Hispanic missing people you've been looking for?"

"Nope." That's the business that had brought me to Vito's lair when the floater turned up.

"What's your take on Jose?"

"I don't know what you're fishing for, but here's what I have. He probably doesn't have a green card, and it would take about five minutes to learn his real name."

"How do you know that?"

"I think his mother saw the pictures on TV or in the papers and wrangled a job scrubbing floors at the hospital to be close to him. She can't say anything for fear she'll get him deported."

"You're good, Trav, I'll say that. The papers didn't overplay your abilities, even if they did lay that 'Blue-Eyed Indian' tag on you."

I could have told him what a cross to bear that had become. We walked side by side down the corridor to his lab. I gave him a sideways glance. "What else is there on Jose?"

"I'll get to that." Vito swung the door open and we went into the room where he spent most of his time. A microphone hung down over a flat steel table. I'd been here through some of the action moments on the table and hoped I wasn't due for another round of that.

He went over to one of the square metal sliding doors along the wall, gave one drawer a tug and we stood out of the way as he pulled it all the way out. There lay Lola Pillaccherosi, pale as some midnight-blooming white flower; but it was her.

I looked down at her face, saw it now in repose as if for the first time. There was something there, something elusive that had been hard to catch when she had her deflector shields up. It hovered like a ghost or wisp, halfway between scared little girl and independent woman. I had caught a bit of it before—it had come through between the words of her singing. It showed there now, more in her relaxed dead face than anything she had shared with me during her life. She no longer looked like just a hard and abrasive person. I could relate to this Lola. She looked a little frail, scared, and very alone. Now she was very dead.

"What's your take on the cause of death?" I could see the bruises I'd seen earlier, but no new wounds.

"Take a look," Vito encouraged. "There was some blunt force trauma first, but that's not what killed her."

I'd seen a lot of corpses in my day, and a lot of obvious causes of death. Nothing here caught my eye, nothing at all.

"Don't keep me guessing," I said. "What's your initial take?"

He pointed to a spot on her neck. I bent over close to the tray, could see two puncture marks an inch-and-a-half apart. "Get outta here," I said.

I don't go to movies at all these days, but when I did I am one of those types who have to say over and over, "It's not real. It's just a movie." I caught *The Exorcist* on a motel TV one night and wished I'd turned the damn thing off. Aside from not sleeping at all that night, I couldn't look any little girl in the eye for quite a spell. Seeing that tiny head spin around and all that gave me reason for an occasional libation even yet. Looking at Lola I could think of nothing to say. "This isn't real" failed me at the moment.

"I'll know more after the autopsy. But I want you to see something else." He moved down to her feet, reached and spread apart the big toe from the next toe on her left foot.

I bent close to look. "A pentagram," I said. "A tattoo. I thought it was illegal for any tattooist to work on the hands, feet, or neck."

"The legality of the tattoo's the least of our worries." Vito slid the tray back into the wall. "Let me tell you about Jose first." Vito led the way. We passed his small office with a paper-cluttered desk that pressed against one wall as he eased me back to the doors where they bring the stiff bodies in at night, and sometimes during the day. I'd seen all I needed to see to get me a whole new set of dreams.

"Jose weighed about a hundred and fifty pounds. That means his body normally holds five thousand milliliters of blood, about five-and-a-half quarts. To cut to the chase, Jose came in at about a quart low."

"He have puncture marks, too?"

"The initial examination missed them. I had a hunch and found them. In addition to whatever other exposure he suffered, his exsanguination . . ."

"What?"

"Loss of blood didn't help him any." Vito glanced over to the wall of square metal doors.

"And Lola?"

"I think she lost even more blood. Way more than she could stand to lose."

"Why are you sharing this with me?" I asked. We stood beside the doors that led outside. Vito and I had been friends a while, but he knew that someone in homicide would be hopping at what he had shared with me.

Vito grinned. "Because you're always the fox in the chicken yard. I know you. You're poking around and you're going to turn this up anyhow. I want you to help keep a lid on it for now. The whole department has asked, well, *demanded* that we keep this away from the press for as long as possible or we're going to have the public running through the streets screaming, 'Vampire.' "

"The floater too?"

"Probably, though it's harder to tell there. A body with a prolonged immersion in water can have a lot of blood leached out by the water through even the smallest of wounds. It's almost impossible to tell."

"But you found the same punctures?"

"I . . . I can't say for sure. I looked, but can't confirm that. But I suspect there were holes there too somewhere."

"What? What else is it you're not saying?"

"That these aren't the first," he said, "or maybe the last. Remember, though. Hush-hush."

"How about the citizens who were there when the bodies were found? How're you going to keep them hushed?"

"They've been told to keep still about it too."

"You think they will?" I said. "That they can?"

"Well . . ." he said, as I swung the door open and saw three media vans pull up and one guy with a camera on his shoulder running through the rain toward us with a trench-coated woman I'd seen on TV running beside him as she held a microphone and pressed an earpiece into place.

"Vito," I said. "My guess is that the lid has come off."

"Completely off," he agreed.

We ducked back inside, locked the doors, and I looked for another way out.

I got out of the car and into the downpour again in front of the gray square stone building behind the main Catholic church building. The church itself ran to gothic lines. I hustled across the damp sidewalk. Sister Consuela had been waiting and swung the door open as I neared it.

"What is it?" I said. I scuffed my shoes on the inside doormat to make up for spraying water all around the foyer. She and the rest of the staff lived and had their offices in this back building. "Did you get hit again?"

For the past six months there had been a rash of small robberies and B & E's all over Austin. The new twist meant that the churches were getting hit as hard as the convenience stores and other businesses. Someone had touched this church for

$2,300 of church donation money only a week back. The story had been in the papers. I'd helped them mount a camera anyway—the usual locked barn after the horse was stolen. Most of the robbed places only got hit once.

"Still keeping the place shut tight?" I asked.

She nodded. "An open door might tempt a saint."

She looked up at me with a round face that could be so calm and placid it made me wonder if there was something to religion. "There's something I want to show you."

Sister Consuela had for some time an enigma to me. She had a farm girl freshness and wholesomeness that appealed to me, but she carried some buried and secret sorrow. I'd asked her once how she came to be a nun. She said, "They didn't have openings for girls in the French Foreign Legion when I was young."

She also had this thing with sayings. She said to me once, " 'You look like a runner,' the devil told the crab." Things like that I couldn't begin to understand. Maybe my understanding what she meant didn't matter.

I followed her down the hall to the back office. The mission's donation box hung inside the door with just a slot outside. I had mounted a camera lens, a small wired-button surveillance affair most people wouldn't notice, where it could record donations, or, in this case, depredations. The video camera itself I'd housed inside. Sister Consuela took a videotape over to a VCR, popped it in, and turned on the television.

She hit the fast forward button and stopped the tape abruptly. Then she let the tape run. I saw an empty sidewalk path, rain beating down on it. A motion sensor had turned on the camera. Feet entered the picture, female feet, then a coat. When she got close enough, I caught the face: Lola Pillaccherosi. Having just seen her a short time before on a slab at the morgue, a cold shudder rattled through my bones. It felt like I looked at a ghost.

Lola looked both ways, then reached out and put an envelope into the collection box. She walked away with crisp, brisk steps.

Sister Consuela stopped the tape.

"What was in the envelope?" I asked.

"Twenty-three hundred dollars," she said.

"The amount was never in the papers or media reports, was it?"

"No," she said, "it wasn't."

By hustling and being a real jerk in traffic, I got back to the office five minutes before Cassie arrived. I turned on the lights, tugged off my damp suit jacket, and thought of going back to fluff up the cot. Too late. She came through the door, wet but still looking as radiant as the Sun-Maid girl on a box of raisins even while shaking half a quart of the great outdoors off her uniform. She had tucked her long blond hair up under her Smokey the Bear hat. She still looked like someone who belonged on the Swedish bikini team instead of a small town's sheriff's department.

I felt the idiot smile, so full of renewed hope on my face, dim as I looked into her face. She nodded, gave me half a feeble smile. "Trav, we've got to talk."

The smile froze, then start to ooze from my face. She looked back at me. The skin of her face was so smooth. Her eyes were the blue of icebergs in the North Sea.

"I know the words," I said, "even if I don't have the sheet music handy. There's someone else."

"Will we be able to stay friends?" I had never seen her face so uncertain.

"We've always been friends," I said. "What d'you say to letting me buy you a burger at Hut's?"

She nodded, not trusting herself with words. I reached for my jacket and slid it back on, moving slowly so as not to rattle all the broken glass inside me.

The razor swept along her inner arm, across the smooth pale tan of her fifteen-year-old skin. The flesh peeled open, as if ripe. A quarter-inch of red, raw meat showed for only a second before the cut filled with blood.

Her father held her trembling arm like a fragile vessel in his calloused hands, his eyes up and staring at the dark figure in the flickering light. Eyes in laser beams glared down at him. His head bent and lowered until his dry quivering lips pressed against the wound, and he sucked deep and long while his daughter made a low moan.

CHAPTER THREE

I did and didn't want to know.

Cassie sat across the booth from me, her very white teeth tearing into a guacamole-bacon cheeseburger with the hearty, lusty appetite that was one of her attractions. I thought about the guy. Who was he? What did he look like? How different could he be from me? I was just mentally getting to the dicey intimate part when she said, "Hey, snap out of it."

The crowd around us looked like the usual packed Hut's noontime offering. Hut's is a '50s-style diner with memorabilia from sports and Texas covering the walls and even the ceiling. You could see enough dust, wear, tear, and stains to let you know it isn't just an act. I usually liked coming here. The food is far from pretentious, is very good, and is priced right even for someone like me who sometimes had to wonder about making rent.

I looked down at my plate where my burger had one small bite missing. Ketchup congealed beside it like a slow wound. I pushed at the ends of a couple of fries that were cooling.

I don't know that I'd pictured us heading for some sort of cottage with white picket fence/cozy couple scenario, but I guess I hadn't gotten all of me to the sense of closure that allowed me to be as graceful as I wished to be at the moment. Looking at her shining radiance, I drifted closer to a mental picture something like the Beauty and the Beast, me playing the part of lesser billing.

She swiped at her mouth with a napkin, then said, "You said we could be friends."

"Yeah," I said. "I'm adjusting."

I think I live out on the edge of the rest of the world at times—had not been too sure how much I would, or could open to real relationship. I thought I'd been warming to the idea. Some of that could have been from sharing the cot. A distant muted trumpet played in a far back corner of my head, competing with a Chuck Berry time-vault song coming from the jukebox.

Folks packed the other tables, crowded the aisles between them as they came and went in a flurry on their lunch breaks.

"You going to eat those?"

"Help yourself," I told her.

I watched her eat, enjoying that at least.

"Joz being my sister makes you uncomfortable, doesn't it?" she said between bites.

Well hell, just knowing Joz at all made me and everyone who considered themselves sane uncomfortable. Joz Brosche might be tiny and flinty, but she packed a lot of punch as a killer. Her husband had been one of the biggest and toughest guys in all of West Texas. One day he came up missing. Most people thought Joz had put him out like a short cigarette.

"What's that have to do with anything?" I said.

"Oh, Trav. You know why I'm still working for Harmon Cuthers. It's because he's the kind of sheriff who's more of a 'peace officer' than a heavy. I'm working on myself. I don't know that you fully understand, or trust that."

"Well . . ." I started to say, then had nothing to add to it. We had been through all this, in both long and short versions.

"What else is haunting those sad bones of your face?" she said, shoving a French fry between her pale pink lips for punctuation. She never wore makeup; didn't need it, which went in her favor with me.

"It's . . . oh, nothing worth . . . it's just a little far-fetched until I get a clearer picture."

"Come on," she said. She ran a napkin across her mouth, left a thin trail of guacamole behind. I reached over, and with one finger swept that off the smooth skin of her cheek and lip, rubbed it on my napkin.

I bent closer to the table and leaned in. "What do you know about vampirism?" I said.

She looked up from the plate where she toyed with her last onion ring. Her blond eyelashes slammed open all the way. "You mean clinical vampirism, I hope."

"Enlighten me."

"The difference is whether you wear a necklace of garlic to bed, or if you think someone is mimicking traits common to those we associate with vampires. You heard about the cases in Florida and Baton Rouge, didn't you?"

"Bits and pieces." Getting onto the details of her job seemed to relax Cassie. I caught some guy at a nearby table checking out how well Cassie filled out her uniform. My blue eyes spun green for a second.

"I'm glad to see," she added, "that you're able to shrug off all this other personal nonsense and focus on business. That's something I've always admired about you."

My lord, I thought, *I hope it's not Harmon Cuthers. That old goat is in his sixties.*

She leaned closer so the people tucking into their burgers at the nearer tables couldn't hear. "In the cases we know about," she said in a low voice, "some involve aspects of necrophilia, sadism, cannibalism, and a fascination with blood. If you follow the lines of the usual diagnostic categories, schizophrenia and psychopathic behavior get high points. Someone with his or her reality that tangled up with myth might have a complex of mother-child dyad, their blood ties in a complete tangle. Now just who do you think is loose who fits any of that?" Her huge, pale blue eyes stared at me without blinking.

"I was just asking," I said. She had lost me early on in the psycho-mumbo-jumbo. I had adjusted some time ago to the fact that a lot of women are smarter than me. Cassie happens to be *way* smarter, particularly when it comes to criminal psychology. I'm more of an old-fashioned cause-and-effect guy.

"Come on," she said. "Spill. Does this connect to that wild dribble I heard on the news on the way here? *Vampires.* Can you imagine? I thought the announcer's prescription medicine had kicked into overdrive."

I leaned closer, didn't want anyone on the other side of our booth to hear the wild shit I was about to share. "A fellow named Armando Ortega, big in the lawn care and maid service business, hired me to look into some of his workers, people who he used, had gone missing."

"Illegals?"

"I didn't ask, but probably. He had gone to the police, but he got the impression that they didn't intend to give it a huge effort, so he came to me."

"Because he knows your heart bleeds and is the size of the capital building?"

"Because he thought I would do something. Anything."

I waited to see if she wanted to butt in again, but she gave me a patient, pale blue-eyed stare as if I was the one having trouble telling the story.

"I asked my friend Vito, who does autopsies and such at the forensics lab, if he'd seen or heard of any bodies coming through. I even found one floater that crossed his desk, or table, rather."

"You did a favor for Vito in the past?"

"Of course. It was personal, but he claims it changed his life, that he owes me."

"Figures."

I told Cassie about Lola Pillaccherosi too, how Owen asked me to help her about what was bugging her, only she didn't want my help, and then she ended up dead with holes in her neck. When I got to the abuse bruises, Cassie's eyes narrowed a notch. For the first time since I'd known her, I saw for a second a glimmer of resemblance between her and her sister, Joz Brosche. Cassie had dealt with far too many heavy-handed men out in her neck of the woods. Her sister Joz had as well, only none of the men she had dealt with were usually ever seen again. Then I mentioned the series of robberies, how that got me helping Sister Consuela at the church, and how Lola's image had popped up again there. When I got to the puncture marks on Lola's neck, and the ones on other bodies Vito had spotted before that, a predatory sparkle settled into the slits Cassie's pale blue eyes had become.

"Why do you think Owen hired you?"

I knew where she headed with that: not too long back, a man who I thought to be an old friend had turned out to be the puppeteer behind the strings while I had rushed around town like a fool in a misguided frenzy.

"Let me explain about Owen," I said. "Lola has been with Owen since he took over the club. His most endearing quality is that he really cares about his performers. He has loyalty. A lot of venues turned up their noses at Up-And-Down Jonesy when his star got tarnished, but not Owen."

I took a sip of my iced tea and wished for something stronger. I said, "Owen might look like some minor figure in an underworld flick, but if you had to sum him up in a nutshell, it would be as a 'cherub.' Beneath the hard shell he uses to get respect running a business, he's one round, furry, and noble-spirited fellow—though he doesn't want that bandied around.

He's always a soft touch for anyone with a good yarn. Everyone in the music biz knows that he overpays his staff. That buys him the sort of loyalty you can get with that. He also gives good juice to the other acts that roll through. I imagine he had a special soft spot for Lola. There are fellows who play it rough in this town who seem to feel that Peasey has some lead in his sock. They hint at stories from his younger days, and Owen doesn't do much to discourage those stories. The yarns help maintain order. But, if you ask me, he's all teddy bear."

Cassie stared at me, right through me, and tilted her head a quarter inch. "Hearing all this as an outsider, it all sounds connected to me."

I started to say something, but she held up the flat of a hand. It was a fine hand, one I would give a lot to hold.

"You have a rash of small robberies that finally extend even into churches. You have a number of missing people, mostly Hispanic, and then there's a string of vampire deaths the police try to keep quiet but fail to do so. Finding a pentagram between Lola's toes is just the sort of icing that cake needed. Now the media is after the sizzle, the sexy vampire or cult worship story, while the steak remains unexamined, or at least doesn't get the scrutiny it deserves. The public's just lucky it has someone with your tenacity and pluck involved who cares deeply about the common person."

"I don't know about that." Her mix of metaphors hadn't lost me, but nothing was clearer than it had been before.

A crowd of people over by the front door waited to get a table. The waitress gave Cassie and me the hairy eyeball for staying too long. I paid up and we ambled toward the door.

Outside, Cassie said, "If you'd like, I've got the afternoon and I can try to get some more time off, pitch in a little. This sounds like a case I could . . ."

I caught the pause and flush of pink. "You were going to say 'sink my teeth into,' weren't you?" The flush turning brighter confirmed the Freudian direction that slip had been taking. "No," I said. "I'll be fine. Besides, you need to be getting back to Kerrville."

"I can spare an afternoon. You could stand to know more about vampires and cults if you're going to be dabbling in a mess like this," she said. She looked right at me, gave me no room to squirm.

"I don't believe in vampires."

"I didn't say you did. Want my help or not?"

"Okay."

"It's another deputy, Trav. The new one who replaced Alvin."

"Hazel?" I'd met the new black deputy. He'd been right with us wading into an Aryan paramilitary camp out in the back woods. My ever-conscious battle with prejudice whipped me for thinking where I'd been going with that.

"No. Another deputy, one who had been already slated to join us just before Alvin went rogue." Her eyes swung to mine. "It's someone closer to . . . my own age. I'm sorry, Travis."

I grinned back at her. At least I know my face didn't fall apart.

We drove in separate cars to our next stop. I wove up through the afternoon traffic with my caseload to keep me warm. The sky had turned the stained battleship gray of one of the rusting hulks in our nation's mothball fleet. The streets were filled with the last independent thinkers in America. At least no one seemed to drive according to any plan or shared agenda that I could make sense of.

I pulled in at the local Barnes & Noble mega-bookstore and Cassie parked beside me. We went in and looked for the information desk. Chairs and sofas had been scattered through-out the store, and a coffee house had opened in the corner.

Whatever the public library used to be, the bookstore these days had taken much of its place. People lounged everywhere, reading magazines and bending the covers of books. How stores like this make money is not obvious to me. But, like everyone else who didn't have the Internet at home, I had learned to use them as research centers.

A young redheaded female clerk, with a tattoo of a barbed-wire bracelet around her wrist, didn't seem fazed by my question and pointed us to the occult shelves. Two young girls giggled over a paper volume on witchcraft, a nineteenth-century reprint from Dover Press. Both girls had very pale white faces, hair dyed black with purple streaks. They had painted their nails black and one girl had shaved her eyebrows and had a ring pierced where one eyebrow used to be. They seemed to get a huge kick out of Cassie's uniform. The occasions on which I'm glad I've never made it as far as parenthood come more often on some days.

A lot of books about vampires filled the shelf. We got the beady eye from the two girls when we scooped up half a dozen of them and took the stack over to the coffee shop. We sat at a small table near the windows, with steaming cups of Mocha Java in front of us. The two coven-wannabe girls sat down at a table near us with their book. They looked up and giggled in our direction from time to time.

Seven cups of coffee and a very long afternoon later, I looked up. It had gotten dark outside. Caffeine raced through me like a bushel basket of Indy 500 cars, along with some other pictures in my head that weren't going to help me sleep. I caught the reflection of Cassie and myself in the window against the black night outside. I looked at Cassie, all blond and smooth, bent over her book, and at myself, all sharp edges, high cheekbones, black hair beginning to get a middle-age unruliness, eyes staring into the glass with matching hardness. What the hell had I been thinking anyway?

Cassie looked up. "Hey," she said, "this stuff we're reading here is mostly folklore. None of it can be as bad as your face looks."

"Thanks," I said. "I was thinking of something else."

"You find anything you can use?"

"This Vlad 'the Impaler' from Romania seems like a nice fellow. Some Turkish envoys refused to take off their turbans during a visit, so Vlad ordered his men to nail the turbans to the envoys' heads."

"Prince Vlad Tepes," Cassie nodded. "The original Dracula. His father was known as Dracul, or the dragon. Vlad became 'son of the dragon,' or Dracula. That's all interesting, but you do know what kind of stuff we're looking for, don't you?"

"Yeah, motivation stuff."

"Right. The kind of things I use in psychological profiles. It's too early to make a lot of assumptions about what you've got. You don't even know that you're really tying into vampirism."

"A lot of people could just have a couple of holes in their necks."

"You know what I mean. It could be masking, someone with other motives trying to confuse an investigation."

"That part's working."

"Anyway," Cassie said, "what I mean is more like the case of Elizabeth Báthory, a sixteenth-century countess in Hungary. She got hooked on the black arts through her manservant, Thorko. One of the countess's maids hurt her while combing her hair with a brush. Elizabeth slapped the maid and it drew blood. Where the maid's blood had splashed on Elizabeth's hand the skin seemed to grow young. Elizabeth convinced herself that the blood of young girls could keep her young. So she started by having the blood of the maid removed and put into a large vat. She bathed in the blood. This went on for about ten years with different young girls. Her nurse and Thorko helped find and drain young girls, until one of the potential victims got loose and ratted out Elizabeth."

"They string her up then?"

"Well, no. They tried and executed the accomplices, but Elizabeth had friends in high places. Her cousin was prime minister. She just got confined to her room."

"Grounded, even way back then. Sounds rough."

"She died four years later, if that makes you feel better."

"You gotta love a fair justice system."

"Don't miss where I'm going with this," she said.

The blank look she saw on my face encouraged her to share more.

"Part of the fascination for some people with all this— particularly young people and those inclined to feel strongly about spiritual matters—is bigger than the fountain-of-youth thing I just mentioned. Some people, occultists, say that a person has a physical body as well as an astral body that's trapped in the physical body. The astral body's the one that, with vampires, stays alive by tapping the basic life fluid of others, blood. I know it seems a stretch, but there *is* some mild support for the rationalization that vampires might exist. You've been around people who seem to sap your energy, leave you feeling tired, haven't you?"

"Like now?" I said, though all the caffeine jogging through me made that a lie.

Cassie glanced at her watch. "Jeez," she said. "I've got to get going." Hearing her say that made me think of Owen Jeezey Peasey. I had to go see how he had taken Lola's death.

"And wipe that Gloomy Gus look off your face," she said. "We're still friends, right?"

"Right."

"Where are you off to?"

"I've got to do a little night-clubbing."

Outside, the black of the night was split by the white flash of a crackling bolt of lightning. Seconds later there was the boom of thunder. Rain began to pour, in big rounded drops at first, then in slanting silvery knives packed in tight sheets. Beyond that, the night was as black as any I'd seen.

"It was a dark and stormy night," Cassie said. She grinned as she said it. She put on her Smokey the Bear hat and went out into the thick of the storm.

MIAMI, Florida (AP)—*John Brennan Crutchley, a former engineer, known as the Vampire Rapist, abducted a nineteen-year-old Melbourne, Florida, girl. He repeatedly raped her, then used an intravenous device to drain and drink her blood. In 1985, after serving ten years of a twenty-five-year sentence, he was released for good behavior from a Florida prison on a fifty-year probation. He is now married and has a son.*

CHAPTER FOUR

The longer I watched the red eyes of Cassie's tail lights recede into the blur of the storm the more it seemed like a good idea to stay inside. Drinking one more cup of black coffee, though, would wind me up tight enough to vote Republican. I gave myself the mental kick in the pants I needed and slogged out to the car in the downpour. The rain felt very cold, and soaked through to my skin three steps out the door of the warm coffee shop. I flopped soggy and soaked into the driver's seat, fired up my sturdy metal shoebox of a car, clicked on the heater at full, and headed for Owen's place. At least the traffic had thinned out. I flipped on the radio, a novelty for me to be in a vehicle where it worked. Folks were calling into a talk show with sightings of vampires all over the city. One had made away with a woman's terrier, Muzzie, she said. Another fellow got into an argument about silver bullets versus wooden spikes. A guy recently back from a combat front had a jumbled plan that involved a flame thrower and .50 caliber cough medicine he planned to give the vampires. It all seemed silly, but at the same time not. The headlines and lead stories had all shifted to this new sizzle.

By the time I had gotten halfway across town the skies shared less thunder and lightning. The rain came steady, though, and the late-night streets had the few cautious drivers on the roads pushing their headlights through the wet in a methodical and slow way. The hands on my tired Timex nudged ten o'clock when I pulled into the lot beside the Devil's Due. Seemed to be plenty of parking places.

Inside the club, Up-and-Down Jonesy mixed with the smattering of a crowd while between sets. Owen spotted me where I stood just inside the door. He wrapped up with the people over whose table he bent and stood upright and rushed over.

"Jeez, my knees, Trav," he said the minute he was up to me. "What have the hell have you been up to? I've had cops in here up to my eyebrows. You'd be surprised how that dampens the gate." He took a large white handkerchief out of the breast pocket of his jacket and swept it across his forehead where lines of moist skin were bunched in rows. He wrestled away the frown, forced a weak smile. "Oh, what the hell. I'm just upset about Lola. I don't mean to bust your chops. What *have* you done so far?"

I looked around the club, tried to see who was here and who wasn't. "Let's go somewhere where we can talk."

He nodded toward the back. I followed. A couple of people at different tables waved for Owen to come over, but he brushed off the invitations. We slipped into the dark hallway and he led us to Lola's dressing room. He flipped the switch as we went in and the lights that circled the mirror came on. There was fingerprint powder all over the place. A couple of the drawers had been left half open, and some of the makeup and other stuff had been piled on the floor.

I turned to him and said, "Owen, most of the time in cases I work on the fringe of where the regular cops and detectives prowl. You know their standard operating procedure as well as I do. They'll be hitting Lola's family, friends, and contacts. All I can hope for is to find some thread they missed if I'm to be of any use to you. I'll be nosing around for that thread. It'll help me to know if anything special has happened here?"

"Except for the cops, no," he said. He glanced around at the tumbled mess the room had become. "I've had them around like some people have mice. You don't have any clout with the boys in blue, do you?"

"I'd hate to have to tell you just how little clout I have. It's more like the opposite of clout."

"Well, jeez, Trav . . ."

I held up a hand. "The cops were here awfully fast the night Lola went on a toot. You know any reason they might be patrolling the neighborhood?"

"There's a methadone clinic just down the street, Trav. It got knocked over a few nights back. The uniforms have been around like flies since then."

While he spoke I looked around the dressing room. I had noticed earlier how little of Lola had been in the room. A glass top covered the counter beneath the mirror and lights. When I had been here last, I'd seen a photograph and a small white business card beneath the right corner of the glass. I reached over and brushed away the white powder the police had left. I didn't see either item there now.

"What is it?" Owen asked. He watched me lift the glass off the countertop and hold it up to the light. I gave one side of it a puff of breath to clear off the fingerprint powder. I turned the glass over and peered close. I couldn't make out anything from where the photo had been. The business card, though, had left an impression where the ink had been pressed against the glass.

"Oh, probably nothing," I said. The word Rostini looked clear enough. I smeared the impression with my thumb until it couldn't be read anymore, then I put the glass back down on the counter.

"You still want me to look into this?" I said.

"More than ever."

"I need a couple of things, Owen."

"Name them."

"I need a name and address on the ex-husband, and I need to know who the well-dressed gent was who sat front row center the other night."

"Jeez, Trav."

"Oh, come on. You already gave this to the cops, Owen. You don't want to hobble me, do you?"

I gave the room another sweeping look, hoping for one more little scrap of a clue from some corner or wall. I saw nothing. I felt Owen's stubby hard hands grab my forearm. I turned to look at him.

He stared up at me, his round face an all-over scarlet tint, and he quivered. His eyes had narrowed to angry slits. He gave himself a moment, then said, between closed teeth, "If I ever find who done this, Trav . . . well, you don't wanna know. Lola was like family, a daughter. You never saw her when she wasn't mad, but she had her sweet moments, especially earlier, when she was getting started. This's a rough biz, Trav. It takes a toll on people."

"Apparently," I said. His claws let go of me, and I felt the blood flow back into my hands.

"Sorry, Trav. It's just that . . ." He reached for his handkerchief again and turned away from me. I made myself busy doing nothing for a few moments.

"C'mon," he said. He took his face out of the handkerchief and waved me toward the door. "I'll get you that address stuff you wanted." His face slipped into a scowl he couldn't hide. If he'd been having a moment of grief, it had shifted quickly enough back to rage. What he wanted now was someone's head on a stick.

"How many chins is a person *supposed* to have?" she asked, and burst into giggles that sent her extra half-chin bouncing. Her head tossed back as she laughed. The curling red thick hair that stuck out from under her scarlet scarf bounced as well.

"Several of yours are quite nice," I said.

That sent her into another flurry of laughter. I looked around the room. Charts of palmistry, phrenology, and astrology covered the dark walls. A large crystal ball on a mount sat in the center of a table off to one side. Beside it I saw a small pile of business cards. The imprint of the card matched the impression I'd seen on the glass in Lola's dressing room. On the table in front of Madam Rostini were two open pizza boxes. The smell of hot cheese, garlic, and pepperoni filled the room. "If I know you come, I order you one," she'd said when I came in. "Touch either of these—you die." Her head tilted back again in laughter. She seemed to amuse herself with ease.

The small room seemed filled with her laughter, and with Madam Rostini. She was quite a departure from the expectations I had when I pulled up in front of her little white cottage with its large Fortune-Teller sign. She looked to be in her late twenties, had the cutest round face, and seemed to delight in thinking she was half a step from statehood in size. There might be a hundred and fifty to sixty pounds to all five-foot-four of her, but I doubted she weighed more than that.

My suit quietly dripped onto the rug centered under the table in the hardwood floor. I could hear the storm outside battering against the white wooden cottage that served as her home and office.

One pink shell of a hand moved over one of the pizza boxes while she laughed. Fingers dainty enough to play a harpsichord plucked a piece of pepperoni, carried it back to her mouth. She looked at me, chuckling while she chewed. All of her but her eyes kept up the mirth I'd seen since entering the room. The eyes, though, pale and hazel, stayed busy flitting across me and into me.

She stopped laughing and sat upright, brushed crumbs off

her jiggling black silk blouse. A string of gold and silver coins that hung around her neck rattled. "But, of course, you are full of pain and questions. Else why would you come to see Madam Rostini?"

"Well," I said, "I didn't really come for a reading. I was hoping for some information."

She wiggled a set of pink fingers at me. "Just stay parked, fella. I get to you." She closed the pizza boxes and moved them to the side table, sweeping the tablecloth with the flat of her hand. "The thing with pizza," she said, "is as good cold as hot. Better than love, no? More like revenge, yes?" She came back to the center table carrying the crystal ball on its stand. She moved in a graceful flow.

"I said I didn't come for analysis."

Her face lifted to mine as she lowered herself back into her chair—a stern face this time. "No one ever does. Is serious, but not. Big joke. Come see Madam Rostini. But most people believe and don't believe. You are surprised, no?"

She brushed her hands off on her skirt, then bent and looked into the ball in front of her. The lights in the room dimmed. I couldn't see if she used a foot pedal or some gadget with her knee. It was a trick, I hoped, and a darned good one.

"I'm working on something and just need a little help, direction," I tried again. "I hope to learn . . ."

"Don't tell too much," she held up the flat of one hand. "Let the Madam discover."

I sighed. Her face went blank as it looked back at me. It would be her stock-in-trade to be able to look ambiguous. She bowed her head to look into the ball. You know, it's kind of hard not to think or even say out loud when you think something like this is a load of rich and fragrant elephant crap, so I struggled but kept my opinions to myself.

"You have . . ." she stopped, looked up at me again, as if

catching a glimpse of me for the first time.

"What?"

"You toy with sinister forces," she said, her small voice growing deeper and more threatening. "You are strong, and alone, very alone. You have weathered much, but worse is to come, before better."

The voice change seemed good. I took her words out of context and considered how they'd hold up as an astrology prediction. About par, I guessed.

"Is okay not to believe," she said. "Most do not, even among those who profess most strongly that they do."

"Hey," I said. "I hope I haven't misled you about . . ."

"You come seeking that which you will not be pleased to find. There are dark forces." She looked up from the ball and into me. Her eyes grew dark, almost black.

"Kinda dramatic, ain't it?" she said. "Oh, shake out whatever of Halloween has crawled into your head. Let me have a good look, dearie." She lowered her face to the crystal again.

She grinned this time. "You are wishing," she said, "you are wishing someone else was here. That she would be amused. But there is pain there too."

"Do you mind if we . . . ?"

"Yes, Madam Rostini must pick at scabs now and again. You may call me Eva if it pleases. If that bothers you less."

This sure seemed fun to her. People must be real putty in her hands most of the time. However, I had places to go, people to see.

"Do not rise."

"Would this work better if I asked a question?" I said.

She looked up at me. "What you want to know is beyond my powers. You deal in darkness. It is not what pleases you, but there you must go. I cannot find what does please you. For now. There is no charge." The fingers of one hand reached up to twirl a strand of her red hair. "You may go, unless you wish to stay and purchase another pizza pie."

"Look," I said. I felt a tired edge to my voice I tried not to show. "I think I weathered the hocus-pocus enough. I'm here because of Lola Pillaccherosi."

"I know."

"One of your cards was in her dressing room," I said. "The police haven't been here to see you about that?"

She shook her head slowly. Her eyes narrowed. "I would tell them, or you, nothing about another client."

"She's dead."

She said nothing. An enigmatic blank look spread the length of her no-longer cheerful face.

"Maybe you can tell me this," I said. "I'd like to know if you know where people interested in the occult hang out, or cluster. You know, vampires, things like that."

"Yes," she said. "I know. But you will find." She took a deep breath, gave a sigh, struggled to work a smile back onto her face. "What I see in you scares me, I do not mind to confess. Go and deal with what you must. I do not wish to profit from you. Go." Her face grew grim and hard. I couldn't make any sense of it.

"You know," I said. "Every once in a while your accent slips just the tiniest bit. I'm not saying you don't have it down very well. But there's just a hint of live oak and maybe spring blue-bonnets there. You grew up in Texas, didn't you?"

"How will knowing that help you?" she said with no accent at all.

"You really think you have a clear picture of what I'm after?"

She had such a pretty face, I hated to see it twist into the scowl she wore. "Before you are done," her words had an echo to them, "you will wrestle with nothing less than the Prince of Darkness."

The tent was too small to hold as many people as it did. Rain hammering against the cloth made them huddle closer together. Wind raged like some beast clawing at the small shelter. Even the children played in a tentative and desultory way. The women gathered around a communal pot, their chatter low and between themselves. Men, with calloused hands and worn muscles, too tired to do more than sit and sip at cans of beer, huddled near the tent flap. The smell of frijoles filled the tent in a way that should have been comforting, but wasn't.

The tent flap swept suddenly open and into the tent, crowding its occupants even farther back from the rain that splattered through the opening In stepped tall men, each dressed in black, the water flowing down across capes that acted as rain slickers. Their faces were long, white as they stared. The children secretly crossed themselves, in imitation of their parents. The men, who had clambered to their feet, stood still, waiting. The breeze from the opening whirled through the tent, putting out the candles, and making the fire under the pot surge into leaping flames. None of this seemed new to any of them. They lived with this every day. It felt like fear itself, manifested into physical form.

CHAPTER FIVE

The drive back through the pounding rain and dark narrow streets to my office-slash-home got me there a little after midnight—as early as I could recall getting home during the past few nights. I eased the car slowly along the front of the place, past the blank glaring glass behind the iron bars of my office window. I saw no parked and waiting cars. I could do without Sergeant Borster. I craved sleep and lots of it.

I drove the car around back and parked behind the building. Puddles spread in varying depths across the breadth of the alley. I slogged through the rain around toward the front of the building. I could taste that metallic, sleep-deprived flavor that only a little of the blue agave seems to cut—that and a luxurious four hours of cot time.

The rain had soaked through my clothes to the skin by the time I got to the front door. I gave a lot of strong thought to knocking together an ark and rounding up animals by twos if this rain didn't let up soon.

A car pulled up beside me, interrupting the rasp of my key sliding into the lock. A searchlight beam swung through the rain and fixed on me, freezing me in place like a deer in the headlights. I turned to the car, kept my hands out where they could be seen. I waited for a voice on a loudspeaker to tell me step away from the door. Someone hollered from the car window, "Hey, get over here and into the car before you drown."

The back door to the unmarked cruiser opened when I got to

it. I popped inside and slammed the door on the rain.

The guy in the driver's seat would have been the one wearing the stripes if they had been in uniform and not plain clothes.

"I'm Fallon Barnett," he said, turned to reach across the seat to extend a hand. The gesture gave me the same jolt he'd have given me if he had pointed a gun toward me. I had experienced routine cop behavior and this didn't feel anything like the usual brand.

I reached and shook the hand.

"Detective Sergeant," he added. "This is Forest Kilgallon." He nodded to the guy on the other end of the front seat. "You may have heard of us. Fallon and Forest. Some of the guys at HQ call us the F-Troop." Barnett chuckled to himself while I shook hands with Kilgallon.

I had heard of them, all right. They could come across as nothing but brown sugar, but they could also be ball-busters when they wanted to be. They had one of the highest closed-file records of any of the homicide detective pairs. A lot of cops with their years on the force go stone-faced. Both of these men, Barnett in particular, had the clear faces of people unable to lie. If the open look of their faces was just a ruse, they were very good.

"What brings you out on a night like this?" I said. All the rain I'd soaked up seemed to be settling in my shorts. I felt clammy, cold, and as uncomfortable as I'd have been in an interrogation room's hot seat.

"You comfy back there?"

"No, I'm not," I said. "Look, you guys aren't the Welcome Wagon. Can we cut to what's on your minds?"

"Not in the mood for social amenities, eh?" Barnett said.

Outside, the rain pounded on the parked car. The only lights inside came from the dash and the streetlight that filtered half a block our way through the rain. I waited.

"You were listed as a witness to the autopsy on the floater," Kilgallon said.

"Oh."

"The floater had no green card," Kilgallon said.

"The floater was a missing person's case," I said. "She's not missing anymore."

"No, she's not, is she?"

"You know we work homicides," Barnett said. "Others on the force think that the rash of small crimes may be tied to an influx of Hispanics without green cards."

I said, "That doesn't seem right. Wouldn't they be more likely to lay low and not make waves?"

"We've heard all about you," Kilgallon said, "how your heart bleeds with the best of 'em. We're not out here on this lovely evening to argue right and wrong. We're just following up on what we do know."

"Which is . . . ?"

"Someone, or something, could be driving them to crime. That the way you see it?" Barnett's smile stayed in place, but the eyes didn't match. They narrowed.

"It crossed my mind. What's the angle with you guys? What did you hope to get out of this conversation?"

"Who's your client?" Barnett said.

"You know I can't tell you that."

"There's no law."

"There're ethics."

"Why don't we drop a name for you?" Barnett said. "It's Armando Manuel de Ortega."

"That's a name all right."

"Your client?" Kilgallon said.

"Go ahead," Barnett added. "You can admit to it."

"And if it is?"

"There are one or two things you should know about him."

"You mean he's not just a legitimate owner of a landscape and maid service business, one of the half-dozen largest in the city?"

"You tell him, Kilgallon."

"Illegal aliens."

"You know, Native Americans have an entirely different spin on this illegal alien issue, since they were living here quite nicely before the white man arrived."

Kilgallon ignored me. "We're reasonably sure that Armando is at the end of a pipeline of a stream of illegal aliens coming in from several coyotes."

"Coyotes are the agents, or pimps, who set Mexicans up for illegal entry," Kilgallon said.

"I know what coyotes are," I said. "Why isn't the INS working this?"

"They are." Barnett flexed his neck right and left. Twisting to look back at me gave him a kink, but he kept his smile in place. The smile made me more nervous than anything they said. "We're interested in homicide. You know that. But that's led us to the series of robberies, other small crimes. As individual crimes they may not seem like much. It's likely that someone, like Armando, is behind the crimes. If so, the take from all that's been going on could be quite substantial."

"If a big sum of money's involved, I'm surprised Borster isn't on the case."

Their eyes connected for the briefest part of a second, then snapped back to me.

"What about Borster?" Barnett asked.

"I was beginning to think he handled more than half the city's homicide cases, at least any with large sums of money in the picture," I said. I may have been catching a cold from the damp underwear. A small shiver rippled through me.

"Is he bent, you're thinking?" Kilgallon said. "I don't know.

But you could say he's very interested in his own retirement. I'm just glad he's not my partner."

Barnett said, "Ned does his job. Anything negative you hear about him you didn't hear from us. It's just that he has a different way of doing his job than we do."

"All we want is results," Kilgallon said.

"Not highly publicized ones, and not results that benefit us personally. Enough said on that?"

"What you have on Armando," I said. "Is it solid? When I checked him he seemed clean."

"He's supposed to," Kilgallon said.

"Put it this way," Barnett said. "I wouldn't hire him to babysit."

"So, she dumped you again, huh?" Jimmy Bravuro held a coffee cup halfway to his lips. He stared out the front picture window of the diner at a day that looked gray, but at least not raining like the previous one. "I don't know why you're surprised." He turned back to me in time to catch my shrug. "You know my uncle, Ping Shoe Rodney, over at the rest home?"

"Don't believe I've had the pleasure," I said.

"Well, he's been a bachelor all his life. So, he corners this old maid living there and says, 'Let's get married.' She says to him, 'Land sakes. Who'd have either of *us?*' "

"You're not helping."

"Just trying to be there for you."

Cars outside honked in some early morning traffic snarl. I took a sip of coffee. Someone had mixed French Roast and hot grease and managed to singe the coffee beans at that. Still, it helped wake me.

"You know, man," Jimmy said, "there're times I wish I could be half as laconic as you. It's okay to talk about this. Might even be good for you. Flow with it."

Looking at Jimmy sometimes you'd never know that he is one of Austin's more successful musicians. Off the stage he looks and sounds like something left behind by the '60s, like an old pair of worn, faded, and patched jeans. Under the lights, though, his intense and emotional singing has the venues packed wherever he plays.

"That's not why I asked you to breakfast," I said. The morning crowd had come and gone. We rode out the pause before the lunch infestation.

"And a fine piece of dining it's been," Jimmy said. "These English muffins are hard enough to be manhole covers if they weren't so small."

"I hear you," I said. "The food's awful, and the portions are so small. Do you mind if we get to business?"

"I know. Lola Pillaccherosi. Ol' Jeezy hired you, huh?"

"He doesn't put out a newsletter or anything, does he?"

"No. But those in the know, *know*, Trav. You know how this business is." He took a sip, made a small face, and put the cup down.

"Not as well as I thought."

"It's just too damn bad you never got to meet Lola when she was fit to be around."

"I've heard that. I only caught the recent version."

"She used to be one of the sweet young new ones—working hard, humble, always there for someone else. She did a cover to one or two of my songs, way back, 'fore she settled into that torch singing act she's known for now."

"What made her . . . ?"

"I mean, she may have been one more warm human being, hungry for success, and with a sense of urgency. But she was a definite cuddle in those days compared to lately. She's been cold as a mother-in-law's kiss."

"When did she . . . ?"

"I don't know what happened, unless it's the burn-out that hits a lot of people in the biz. Sometimes you're out in some faraway . . ."

I let go of my coffee cup and held up the flat of a hand. "It's not being laconic," I said, "when I can't wedge a word in edgewise."

"Well." Jimmy gave me a huffy look. "Excuse me all to roller skate." He lifted his cup, and found the coffee cool. He waved the cup toward the counter. Phyllis, who was working the counter and the tables, saw his wave. She picked up the pot off its warmer and started around the counter in our direction.

"What do you know about Up-and-Down Jonesy?" I said.

"You think he's a suspect?"

Phyllis refilled our cups and went over to another table to take an order.

"I didn't say that."

"Well, I know you'd better never call him by that name to his face. His first name is Darrell," Jimmy said.

"I know that."

"You know about his third and fourth CDs then, too."

"They were that bad?"

"They barked at the moon. I mean they really did. It was hard to believe they were made by the same person who made the first two."

"Why didn't someone—his manager, or someone from the record label—help him?"

"He wouldn't let them. This part's harder to understand if you're not in the biz. You get your head down working on something and the ol' muse seems to be sitting on your shoulder. Still, you sometimes have to let a song sit and cool a while before you go back and see if it had anything to it, if it holds up for others."

"And Jonesy wasn't patient enough?"

"Not by a long shot." Jimmy looked up at the wall clock. "Look, man, I got to shake it loose. Anyway, you better wrap up whatever you're working on within the next two weeks if you need any help with the music biz part of it. Me and the musical marines are off to Amsterdam for a two-week hitch. They love us in Amsterdam. What's on your dance card for today?"

"A funeral."

"Well . . . enjoy."

The sky looked as dark gray as the slate of an old-time schoolroom's chalkboard. The faces of the mourners seemed pale against it. Six men lifted Lola's casket from the hearse. One of them was Watt Stoner, her ex-husband. They carried it to where a small crowd stood on a strip of carpeting under a small striped canopy beside an open hole in the ground.

I had missed the funeral ceremony at the church, but had caught up with the procession at the cemetery. There were quite a few people, some the idle curious, most people who had known Lola, or claimed they had. The crowd spread out across several surrounding grave sites. I knew only a few of those present.

Conspicuous by his absence was L. Leroy Hunt, the fellow in the suit I'd seen in Owen's place getting the special singing treatment from Lola. I did see Madam "call me Eva" Rostini. She looked good in black. Sister Consuela helped with the rites. Owen stood by himself in the tangle of people. In the distance, on a hill looking down on the crowd, stood Sergeant Barnett and Detective Kilgallon. Some cops believe a killer will attend a funeral, others don't. It's always good form to attend yourself and have a look.

Sister Consuela stood close to the casket. I moved through the fringe of the crowd, edging closer. I caught Eva's eye for a second, but she looked down into the waiting grave. Owen looked up when I moved to stand beside him. His face showed no sorrow, only a smoldering anger that made me wonder again about those stories of him being connected. He looked a question at me. I shook my head. He looked away.

Some of the loneliest times I've ever had are in the middle of crowds.

Sister Consuela stared hard at the casket, as much question as sorrow on her face. Her back was stiff, her knees locked. She swayed on her feet, tottered forward. An acolyte rushed forward to catch her before she fell sideways into the hole. She shook her head and pushed him gently away, then gave a curt nod that let the rites continue. I looked at Eva again, thought she glared at me. Then I traced her eyes to a young man in an Armani suit who stood facing the same direction as Owen and myself. I could see part of his lean face. He had his long black hair tied back in a ponytail. The man's eyes lifted up to lock with hers a couple of times.

The ex-husband, Watt Stoner, lifted his stare from the casket to look over our way too. His eyes blinked, his mouth tightened. He looked away. I hadn't placed young Mr. Ponytail yet, but he did not seem to be popular among this crowd.

I don't know as much as I should about Catholic funerals. I know I drifted in and out of more Latin than I had been prepared to hear. Once you have exhausted what Latin appears on small change, I am pretty well tapped out on dead languages.

A woman behind us had one of those nagging, slightly irritating coughs that sounded like a small bone might be caught in her throat. She'd start a small series of muffled hacks, then rip to a controlled halt that was only a pause before she started over. A few heads swung back that way to give her a glare she didn't deserve.

"Jeez," Owen said softly when the woman started choking again.

In front of Owen and myself, and standing next to the slim man in black, an equally slender woman in a long black dress with a small black hat and veil turned to look back into the crowd.

A breeze swept across the crowd as she turned. It lifted the veil and let us have a good look at her face.

Owen took a sideways and backwards step, bumping into me. "Jeez, oh, jeez," he said loud enough to turn a few heads.

The woman tugged her veil back into place and turned back toward the front.

"Lola," Owen said to me. I had seen the face too. "That was Lola," he said.

Sturdy white nylon rope bound the girl. She lay on her side on the stone floor. Her hands had been tied behind her back, and the rope from there ran in lines that wrapped around her ankles, in a loop behind her knees and behind her neck. A strip of silver duct tape covered her mouth. She tilted her head up at the tall men by twisting and straining her neck. Wide white rings surrounded her brown eyes in the light brown face that had a look of raw terror. Her long dark hair tossed as she tried to struggle loose.

"Tried to escape?"

"Yeah."

"Make an example of her. Tonight would be good."

"But until then?" One of the men looked down at her housekeeper uniform. The skirt had slid up, revealing a white camisole that clung to her rounded hip. The man picked up the long dagger off the altar. He slid the tip under the fabric of the camisole and slit it all the way open, framing smooth light brown skin. "No one says it has to be a virgin sacrifice," he said.

"Just make sure she's still got a little kick left. These folks do love a ritual."

CHAPTER SIX

From what I could hear over a low murmur in the crowd, the ceremony seemed headed for closure. The lone voice droning in Latin went up half an octave. Some of those in the crowd fidgeted. I fought the urge to tap the woman on the shoulder, get her to turn again. Her slender shoulders had lifted in tension. She moved a half step closer to the slim man. A few people in the crowd still gave us looks. Owen kept grabbing at my arm and nodding. I held up one forefinger.

As soon as the ceremony finished, those who felt the need took turns tossing handfuls of dirt down onto the lowered casket. Owen pushed forward through the shifting crowd. There was enough confusion in the crowd for us to make progress, even though the woman moved away from us. She became separated in the crowd from the man with the ponytail. Owen reached out and grabbed at the woman's bony shoulder. "Lola?" he said, a little louder than I liked.

She spun and faced Owen. The wind lifted the veil away from part of her cheek and one eye, showed a face very pale against the black veil. Her brown eyes grew wide. The expression she wore could have been surprise, could have been fear. Some of the people in the crowd moved toward the casket, others to their waiting cars. Those nearest stopped to watch.

"It's okay," the slim woman said. She tugged the veil all the way clear from her face. To Owen she said, "I understand. But I'm not Lola. My name's Lila."

Owen froze where he stood and stared. So did most of the other people near enough to see her. She looked enough like Lola to be her stunt double.

"Have you ever given thought," Owen said, with none of the grief or anger I had seen on his face, "to being part of the entertainment business?"

Over the heads of those nearest us I saw the detectives head down from their remote spot to mingle in the crowd. They steered toward Lola's ex-husband, Watt Stoner, who, as soon as his duties were over, started toward the line of parked cars. He glanced back over his shoulder and moved even quicker.

Perhaps Fallon and Forest hadn't been able to reach the ex-husband for an interview yet.

The shuffle of people and general confusion following the ceremony continued around us. Owen and Lila stood face to face. The slim man with her pushed his way through the crowd toward her. From the other side of the blur of bobbing heads I saw a head of red hair coming in our direction. Eva.

She stopped a dozen feet away from us, gave me a low hand motion at the end of an arm held stiffly down at her side. She was waving for me to come to her.

I eased close to Owen, gave his thick upper arm a squeeze, and whispered, "I'll get back to you later. I need to see what's up with the ex."

I pushed through the surging crowd, dodged Eva when she pressed close. I slipped around her, hopped over the ankle and shin she extended to trip me.

Watt Stoner broke into a fast walk and hopped into his car, a low-slung silver Acura. He pulled out into the flow of traffic leaving the cemetery. I slipped into a jog and got to where I'd parked my car near the end of the row. Half a dozen cars pulled out in front of me. One of them was the unmarked police car with Sergeant Barnett at the wheel. Some of the vehicles ahead of me were those big, blockish recreational vehicles with tinted windows, impossible to see around. I lost the silver car in the stop-and-go traffic of cars merging out onto a road that had hills and bends in both directions. I saw Barnett and Kilgallon turn left, take a chance he had gone that way. I turned my car right and pushed down on the gas.

The road had enough lanes for me to be obnoxious about weaving between cars to get closer to the head of the pack. Half a dozen miles from the cemetery I caught a glimpse of Stoner's car. I had been the lucky one, not the homicide detectives.

The road got wider and busier. Watt took a ramp that led to an access road. Once on that he took a fork that led to a road that wove into a residential area. When we had gotten far from the cemetery crowd, his pace slowed.

The gray sky grew darker. I flipped on the car's lights, hung back farther so he wouldn't sense a tail. Watt wove through streets until there were fewer and larger houses.

I'd been through the neighborhood before. The soup and cracker crowd did not live here. This crowd went all the way to lobster Newburg. I tried to get a feel for what went through Watt's head after the funeral. Owen had given me Watt's home address. To get there you'd have to go off in the direction the detectives' car had gone.

Watt slowed, then stopped near the iron grill of a gated property. The grounds went on a ways back, far enough I couldn't see the house from the road. I knew who lived there, L. Leroy Hunt. Owen had supplied his address, Lola's well-dressed fan.

Watt pulled over and parked. I ducked into a driveway on the left, turned and went back to park in the other direction. I turned off the lights and sat. I could just make out his car in the rear view mirror. I waited, but he didn't get out of the car.

This went on for an hour. His car started up abruptly and pulled away. I saw the flicker of red tail lights in the mirror, then the car disappeared.

I fired up my car, spun the wheel, and hurried after him. He moved very fast again. I caught up, then stayed back a distance. This time he seemed headed for Lola's place. When we got to the neighborhood he drove past her house, the one he had once shared with her. It had gotten too dark to see the lush green of the Astro-Turf lawn, but I could make out the smooth surface.

The boulevard wove along through homes with lights on, security systems in place, all two or three cars in the garages. Then the road turned into the sharp edges and many cul-de-sacs I had noticed during my last visit, back when Lola was still alive.

Watt slowed his driving. He made a series of right turns. When he had gone around the same block twice and had started a third lap I pulled into one of the cul-de-sacs and nosed my car behind someone's Town Car parked at the curb. Then I sat. Watt's car made two more circles around the block, finally pulling up and stopping.

On a corner lot, and far back up on a hill, a house stood that had Victorian lines in its silhouette against the sky. I looked closer, revised that to gothic lines. It looked like a new house, but someone had read their Poe. The Usher brothers would have been right at home. The blank second-story windows looked like eyes watching down over the other homes.

We sat like that for another hour. Then Watt started his car and left.

I reached for the key and took my time. Night had settled in. It had gotten as dark as the inside of a cow, and I was alone. Nothing new there. I drove slowly, but Watt still sat in his car in his own driveway by the time I got to his house. I didn't spot the unmarked police cruiser in the area. I could see movement in Watt's car. My hand slipped under my seat, grabbed the bag I'd picked up on the way to the funeral. I got out of the car slowly and went to the driver's side. I opened the door.

Watt looked up at me, startled, his face a sheen of wet. I held out the sack. "Can I buy you a drink?"

We sat at an unfinished oak table in the kitchen. He held an empty glass in one hand. His eyes locked on an upper far corner of the room.

"She was a shrewd person, but not necessarily a smart one," he said. It seemed a candid way to speak of an ex-wife he had just seen lowered into the ground.

It had taken the better part of the bottle to get him relaxed enough to talk. I had gotten somewhat relaxed myself.

His eyes looked tired, red. Women probably found him handsome. The chiseled sharp lines of his face still held a boyish quality, though he was nearing thirty. But the strain of the last few days showed as well.

He had turned on every light on the way in, the way a person will when he's not ready to face being alone.

"How do you mean that?" I said.

"She was clever, conniving, Machiavellian, whatever you want to call it. But she was no rocket scientist."

"You have a funny way of mourning."

The kitchen had been left pretty much the way it came. There were the appliances and the walls. Except for the unfinished oak table and chairs, the room looked stark. You could say it had a Spartan manner. The whole house had a hollow, empty quality, barely lived in.

The bottle, in its pushed-down paper sleeve, sat on the table between us. He had rinsed out two mismatched glasses for us. He glanced at the bottle. I nodded. He poured himself another finger of tequila, tossed it back and shuddered. If I had offered to drive a spike into his forehead he would have said to go ahead.

"She was the worst thing ever to happen to me. But also the best. I loved her very much. Still do." He reached for the bottle again without asking.

He looked like the kind of fellow who'd been captain of his football team in high school, an athlete—handsome, with all the girls coming around, his choice of them. Some of the confidence that went with that had been pulled from him like a bad tooth. A weakness, some splinters of fear had crept into his features. Whatever had caused it hadn't emasculated him, but it had taken his edge away. Life had nicked and frayed the corners of his square-faced clean looks. Everything about him seemed assertive except flickerings of uncertainty in his face, and that could be grief. His mouth had gone a little soft and his eyes moved in uncertain darts around the room. He had to rally for scraps of his old self-confidence.

"Have the police been to see you?" I asked.

"They will. I'm a suspect. Every ex-husband is, in something like this. I've just been on the move for a few days."

"They cut out after you from the cemetery. Were you dodging them?"

"No. I didn't know . . ."

"What were you up to? You stopped at a couple of houses."

"You were trailing me?"

"You didn't see me back there?"

"I'm new to . . . all this sort of thing."

"You kind of dodged the question. Leroy Hunt's house and the other one. What was that about?"

"If she'd have just . . ." He stopped mid-sentence and stared.

"What?"

"Been more patient, stayed away from . . . I don't want to go into all that."

"You pretty much have to after putting it that way. You will, anyway. If not to me, then to the police. You're sending up a flag that's only going to excite them."

"You wouldn't understand. No one would." His eyes flicked around the room and settled on the bottle. I was in no position to criticize him for that.

"When did you notice a difference in her? Was there some point where she changed?"

"She was lashing out at people, her agent, me, everyone. She hooked up with some old chums of hers. Then she was calmer, for a while."

"Drugs?"

"I wish. No. It was something else. We had separated by then. I didn't see her at all for a while, then only now and again."

"Like the other night?" The one where Lola had dented my fender and he had slipped away.

He swallowed. A hand that no longer trembled reached for his glass, tilted it to his lips, milked a thin sheen of tequila from the bottom. "Yeah," he said. "Like that."

"Her career meant a lot to her?"

"Everything. She would do anything for it. Anything."

One minute he was looking straight at me, albeit with blurry eyes. Then his head drooped slowly forward. I couldn't make out what he tried to say next. It could have been another mumbled "anything."

I reached over and jiggled his shoulder. He snapped upright in his seat, stared at me. "What?"

"Was Lola superstitious?"

His eyes swept from his glass to the bottle, then back to me. His words were slurred, but clear enough for me to understand. "She was raised Catholic. Astrology interested her later. She was a Gemini."

"She have a twin?"

"No. But she thought she did. That was her biggest . . ." his words were fading. "Fear."

"She feared she might have a twin? I don't get it?"

"No. A doppelganger. She . . . feared . . . that." His head lowered to the table. Blubbery snores pressed out from his slack lips.

I stood up, slid the sack up over what was left of the bottle and slipped it into my pocket. No sense leaving him with any temptations. Odds were good that his nap would be interrupted by homicide detectives.

While he dozed, with his face stayed pressed against the raw oak grain of the dining table, I walked through the rooms of his house. I opened drawers, cabinets, looked into a couple of completely unfurnished rooms.

The house felt as empty as my hopes and dreams. A bare minimum of furniture, clothes, and the bric-a-brac of everyday life formed a skeleton reflection of his life. I would have been sadder for him if his place didn't occupy far more space than my own humble digs. I left Prince Charming to sleep off the potion.

The shift was changing at St. David's Hospital. Automobile lights flicked on here and there across the parking lot. Other arriving cars nosed around looking for places to tuck in for the coming graveyard shift. I watched the faces coming out the employees' door, saw Ginny, my nurse friend, plod out to her car after a day of the kind of work she may have once craved, once thought noble. Now she moved with less enthusiasm, as if rolling sideways out the back of a slow truck. We all have dreams about our jobs. Here I sat staring out of a cooling car with the taste of liquor squirreling around in my mouth. I was nobody's poster boy for Jobs-R-Us.

I had to wait longer than I expected. My quarry must have

stayed on to spend time with her son. As night got a good grip on the parking lot I heard mockingbirds flutter and chirp at each other across the lot. In Texas we have them like some folks have mice. They're the state bird, contrary to those who still argue that the national bird of Texas is the armadillo.

She came out the door, head bowed, as humble and hopeless as any person I'd ever seen. I hated to be the cause of more grief to her, but I turned the key and felt the car's mechanical stir of life. I eased out of the slot and pulled over until I was beside her. I rolled down the window. She had been headed toward the bus stop.

"*Señora. Espere, por favor. ¿Cuándo sale el próximo autobús?*"

Her head snapped to me, but she hurried instead of slowed.

"*Su hijo,*" I said, rolling along to keep pace with her. "*Me no la Migra. ¿Habla inglés?*" I was tiring of not speaking well, and it seemed to do little to comfort her.

She slowed, looked at me and the car, tried to measure what kind of trouble I might be.

"*Sí,*" she said. "*Un pocíto.*"

"*Bueno,*" I said. "Let me give you a ride home. I know about your son. I am not with *La Immigración.*"

I don't know how much of it she bought, if she just wanted to make sure I didn't expose her son, or if it was my smiling face on a cooling evening that made up her mind. She motioned me to stop and came around, got in at the passenger side.

"Where do you live?" I said.

She hesitated, then pointed southeast. That was no surprise. The bulk of Austin's Hispanic population lives in the southeastern portion of the city. It's one of the most liberal cities in the nation, but it still has its "other side of town."

I drove and she never gave an address. She gave a direction every time I needed to turn. We wove down through the darkening streets, lights coming on, neon proclaiming "*Comidas.*"

"Is there hope for your son?" I said. "Does he improve?"

She shook her head, turned her face away from me. I started to feel real swell about this. I had thought out a whole line of questions. In the face of her suffering, they suddenly seemed to mean very little. I kept quiet, let her give me the occasional direction as we wove through the part of the city I didn't know as well as I should.

We went farther and farther into the outskirts of the city. Some of the buildings looked like dark hulks now. An occasional car drove by, its insides crowded with people, possibly gang-bangers looking for a good drive-by shooting opportunity. Gang markings—advertising, the gangs called it—had been scrawled in spray paint on the corner buildings of every block. The markings completely covered one boarded-up house where the owner had given up and moved on. This was no place for a gringo, or a *cabron*, to be at night, especially walking alone on the streets. It felt good, and safer, to be in the car.

She sat still in her seat now, like riding the bus. Her head lifted up, that rare combination of a proud bearing in the face of a humble background I find intriguing, even mysterious. I did not expect to get much from her. She knew about the same as the people who had stood beside me at the intensive-care window watching as their son died. *Nada.*

"*Aquí,*" she said abruptly. "Here, *por favor.*" We weren't near anything.

I pulled over and let her out.

"*Gracias.*"

"*De nada.*"

She stood on the curb, waiting until I pulled away. When I had gotten a block down the street she began to move. I swung into a back street, pressed on the gas, managed to get down a block below her along the way we had come. I eased the car out until I could see her. She glanced back to where I had disappeared before she cut into the lot of a business we'd passed.

A rusting metal sign swayed in the wind at the front of the fenced-off lot. The corrugated metal fence rose high, to hide the smashed autos piled in rows. The sign said: Eddie Paul's Wrecks.

Two men came out of the gap into which the woman had passed. Each held a red can of Tecate beer. They started to sit down on the curb, paused when they saw my car roll slowly to them. I eased to a stop, let them see I was not a cop.

"Is this where I come in the morning if I want to pick up help for my farm?"

They moved closer to my car. The prospect of making a few dollars put some sparkle in their eyes, that or they caught the dim streetlight better closer to me.

They introduced themselves. One was a mestizo from Michoacán, the other a zapotec from Oaxaca. The subject of green cards did not come up. The mestizo, Freddie, he called himself, leaned his elbows on the window of the car and shared some of his beer breath. His zapotec friend stood and glanced up and down the street.

"What are you watching for?" I asked Freddie. He spoke for the two of them. His friend said nothing, perhaps spoke no English and only understood bits and pieces.

"There have been disappearances. You know." A small leather pouch on a leather thong hung from his neck in the V of his open shirt collar. A few beads and a feather had been tied to the pouch.

I pointed a finger toward it. "Does that help?"

He reached and tucked it back into his shirt. "The others," he nodded back to the auto wreck graveyard, "will be here, oh, five, six tomorrow. Early. Look for us two. Okay?" In the distance behind him I heard the low sounds of a radio, probably a battery-run boom-box radio. One of the *norteño* ballads played, weaving a story of underground life in the U.S. in heroic terms.

"You won' forget, will you?" His bloodshot eyes pleaded for work.

"No," I said. It wasn't a lie, but I didn't feel all that good about it. I would remember them, all right. I could only hope someone else gave them work for the day.

The two of them moved back from the car, lowered themselves to the curb. Freddie gave a small hopeful wave.

There would be a lot of them back in there, burning low fires to keep warm, sleeping on the upholstered seats of the smashed autos, money sewn into the hems of their clothes against shakedowns.

I made a U-turn on the deserted street and headed back toward the brighter lights of the city. The bottle made an uncomfortable bulge in my side pocket. I hauled it out, unscrewed the top, took a sip, a toast celebrating the name of the place. I don't like to drink and drive, but I would already melt any Breathalyzer if it came to that.

I didn't know that I'd accomplished anything, or that I knew much more than I had. That's when I heard and felt the dull slam of metal into metal as a bullet plowed into the passenger door of my car. That was no drive-by pistol shot. That was a heavy caliber sniper rifle. I didn't stop, or even slow. The floorboard was the only thing holding the gas pedal back as I pressed hard and got the hell out of there.

"What exactly are we looking for? I mean, all of a sudden there are illegals all through this town."

"There're five million that we know of living in United States. That's not what makes this situation different."

"Then what . . . ?"

"It's how they're getting here, and who's controlling them."

"Someone working the strings, and . . . protection money?"

"Miles."

"What?"

"You're not paid to do the thinking here. So shut up."

CHAPTER SEVEN

I turned the key in the lock of my place. Not quite midnight yet, nor did it rain. The briefest sliver of hope rippled through my tequila-infested brain that things were on a slightly upward curve.

A long time back the Southern Cheyenne believed that the destruction of the white race would take place in a sea of mud. The surface of the earth would become a mire in which the whites would sink, while the Indians would remain on the surface.

For a while during the past few days I had begun to wonder if there was something to that old story. The Indian part of me wondered whether I'd be a sinker or floater. The part I felt in the pit of my stomach, and in my conscience, made me ponder getting a life vest.

I swung the door open, glanced each way down the dim street, even checked the metal grates outside my office picture window. Inside I turned on the lights and reached for the side pocket of my jacket, put what was left of the elixir on the desk.

A small puddle began to form on the hardwood floor beneath me. The dry wood soaked at the puddle. In seconds it had become a dark, moist smear. I peeled off my suit jacket and draped it over the back of the chair.

I heard a knock at the office door. The blinds were down. After the paramilitary fellows had kicked down my old door, my landlord, Les Bettles, had replaced the door with a solid oak model with a mail slot and peephole. I went over to the hole and peeped out.

I unlocked the door and swung it open. "Come on in." Not obsequious, just polite. "I was about to give you a call."

Armando Manuel de Ortega entered my office. The small room seemed suddenly smaller. Armando stands five-seven and I doubt if he goes over one-hundred-fifty pounds. He makes up in venom what he lacks in bulk. He has what some people call sleepy eyes. The lids are always halfway down. He tilts his head back to compensate and his eyes beam in intense glitters. It adds to the native arrogance he carries, gives him a menacing look, not that he needs to be any more threatening than he already is. Until the talk with Barnett and Kilgallon I had thought it might be just an act.

"You gotta tiny place here. Live here too, dontcha?" His voice came out soft, each word a breathy whisper. It made the word "you" sound like "jew," each J sound soft and sinister. He looked around the office. The front room is small—the desk fills a third of it. The back room is smaller. There's barely room for the cot pressed up against the bathroom door. The bathroom is tiny too, only a small stand-up shower, sink, and toilet.

"I hope you didn't expect my place to be on the 'Rich and Famous' tour," I said. "What brings you out so late, Armando? Didn't you get the call I left on your machine?"

"Wha' you wan' to quit on me for? Rocio, you find her for me." I had heard Armando speak before when his accent slipped a couple of times. This was the voice he used when he wanted to be the heavy, downplaying his intelligence, putting his emphasis on muscle.

"She didn't drown, if that's what you mean. She was dead before she ended up in the water." That was the floater I found, and as a reward got to see Vito open and explore.

"So?"

"You aren't involved in her death, are you?"

" 'Course not, pendejo."

"Look, you know where she is. Find someone else to locate the others you told me about."

"I wan' to know why you change you mind. You don' like to work for Armando no more?" His eyes swept the room, panned back to lock with mine.

"I said in the message that I had other cases. I'm just too busy. There are plenty of other detectives. Some almost as cheap as me. You don't have to pay for my locating Rocio if you have a beef."

"You just get these many other cases?"

"Do you have trouble with the concept of 'no'?"

"I want *you* to find them." He stepped close to me, into my space, looked up into my face.

"And I'm saying no."

"*I* decide should you say yes or no. *I* decide you stay on case." His black eyes glittered under the half-hooded lids. His lips pressed tightly together.

When Armando first came to me, he told me he was a businessman. I had doubts then, but the missing people seemed harmless enough. It had turned into an all-Hispanic affair. He had mentioned nothing about green cards, or members of his staff not having them. He hadn't been throwing his weight around like a member of the Hispanic mafia then, either.

He wore a pale green shirt, darker green tie, brown suit jacket, and khaki pants. His hand went inside the jacket.

"If that's a gun you're going for, you had best not."

"Why?" He drew out a gun as he spoke, let it hang down at his side to give his words more emphasis.

"Because I'd have to shoot you." The female voice came from the door to the back room. Cassie stepped out of the darkness. She wore a white blouse, black vest, and jeans tucked into red

91

cowboy boots. Her arms were extended, both hands holding her revolver the way they teach you at Quantico, the way she had learned at the National Academy at the FBI training center where she had been sent as the honored deputy of her department. Her marksmanship scores had been very high.

"Wha' gives, man?" Armando's eyes stayed half-closed, but they looked surprised. He moved back a step toward the door.

"Put it down on the floor," Cassie said. "Slowly."

Armando did as he was told, but he didn't look happy about it.

"You look surprised," Cassie said to me. "Aren't you glad to see me?"

"Always," I lied.

She did look great. Her clear, smiling fresh face with her long blond hair pulled back in a ponytail. She loved this stuff. This fondness of hers for the gunplay, something she had in common with her sister, Joz Brosche, is part of the wall between us. I knew that now. I also had never gotten as fond of her rescuing me as I should be, either. Maybe there were damsels in distress back in King Arthur's time who resented being rescued, too, for all I know.

"What's with you?" I said to Armando. "You said you ran a landscaping and maid service company. All of a sudden you try to go heavy on me."

He had switched to all smiles now. His eyes flicked to the unwavering gun in Cassie's hands. "You can put tha' down. I ain't goin' nowheres." He made short sideways steps toward the door.

"Better stay put, Armando," I said. "I've seen her shoot."

He had to know she wouldn't shoot an unarmed civilian. He could make a bolt for the door at any time and there was little we could do, even less I cared to do. "Go ahead and take a powder," I said, having thought it over.

He reached over to the cord. He opened and closed the blinds—some kind of signal. I glanced at Cassie, moved to the middle of the room and bent to pick up the gun Armando had put on the floor. Cassie's eyes narrowed. Her gun stayed pointed at Armando.

The door handle turned. The door swung open. Armando's smile shifted to a leer. The corners of his mouth snapped back downward, though, when Joz Brosche entered.

Armando rocked back. He'd been expecting his own guys, not Joz.

She doesn't look like much if you have never seen her in action. I had. All I could think of was scorpion, rattlesnake. There she was, maybe five feet tall, tops, with long dirty blond hair, eyes in a permanent squint, her face tanned a saddle brown. I doubt if she weighs a hundred pounds, and that's counting the two or more guns she carries. Her hands were empty. One gun would be tucked behind her back, another into her belt at the front, hidden by her vest. She might have a backup tucked in either boot.

Armando stared at her lean, bony face. She wore a plaid shirt with pearl buttons and jeans, looked like so much flint on the hoof.

"You oughta talk to those men of yours," she said to Armando. "They seem to be chronic nappers." I felt relieved to hear she hadn't cluttered the street in front of my office with any corpses in her usual style.

"*Chupame mi pinga,*" he said, and tried to spit on my floor. But it came out as a dry *pfut.*

"Have to go back to the car for my tweezers and magnifying glass," Joz said. "How's tricks with you guys, Trav, Cassie?"

Armando stared at the gun I held. I removed the ammo, dropped the bullets onto the floor. They made hard clicks as they bounced onto the dry wood and rolled. I held the empty gun out to him. "Mr. Ortega was just leaving, Joz. You mind seeing that he gets to his car?"

"In one piece, Joz," Cassie added.

Armando took the couple of steps to me and snatched the gun. Instead of moving toward the door, as I could have recommended, he bent and made a grab for some of the bullets I'd dropped. His left hand got an inch from the floor when Joz bent to one boot and snapped a hand. A stiletto quivered where it stuck into the wood of the floor. Its point had pierced the web of flesh between Armando's thumb and forefinger.

He stared at the knife, watched as a thin rim of red formed around the edge of the blade.

"I was afraid you weren't going to take Joz seriously," I said. "A lot of people don't at first."

Joz bent forward and wiggled the blade loose from the floor, pulling it out of his hand. She kicked the bullets across the room with the toe of her boot while she wiped the blade on her jeans before slipping it back where she got it.

Armando stood slowly and dropped the empty gun into his jacket pocket. He took out a handkerchief and wrapped it as tight as he could get it around the spot. When he looked up he tried a glare on Joz, then changed his mind and looked away. He held his hurt hand with the other one and sidled around Joz to get to the door. He tried to hide it, but the look he gave her lacked anything like courage. He swung the door open, slipped through and moved off with haste without looking back. Joz followed right behind.

The door closed behind them. Cassie slipped her gun back into its holster at the small of her back. It was just the two of us. We looked at each other.

"How did you know I might need some help just now?" I said.

"Didn't. Just lucky we happened by."

"What are you doing back in town?"

"Man, you really aren't glad to see me."

"I didn't say that."

"I didn't come here to argue with you, Trav. I'm here to help. Maybe I'm asking for more resilience from you than you're capable of, but I doubt that. The focus and simplicity of your life amazes me. You have no hobbies, except that cologne you've been sipping. You just work."

"Am I supposed to be flattered, or upset?"

"I'm trying to understand you. What I'm saying is that I know how hard it is for you to work as a team, even though you have friends."

"Why does that make me feel like some sort of social cripple?"

"You know, you were more polite when the bed was involved."

My mouth opened, closed. There was nothing to say to that.

"You've got to admit that you've spent most of your life avoiding emotion."

I realized I stood with my arms crossed. I uncrossed them and moved to sit on the corner of the desk. I said, "You're afraid that if you become some part of my life it'll take the starch out of me?"

"There's plenty enough starch. I told you before. There's someone else. Get over that. Can we still be friends? Can you accept my help?"

I didn't say anything.

"You don't want us in on this, do you?"

"I didn't . . ."

"You don't have to say it. Is it Joz, or me?"

Whatever cloud had not let me see the big picture earlier lifted as she spoke and I looked at her. For the first time I saw her for what she was. Earlier my judgment had been suspect. Like her sister, Cassie was a warrior. She stood firm, eager, like a knight ready to go on a quest, or Attila the Hun all set for a raid. Seeing her clearly like that gave me relief I didn't need to explain to myself.

The door opened and Joz came back in. She looked as unruffled as if it was just to put the cat out.

"Did you play nice?" Cassie asked.

"They drove away. I didn't put them in the dumpster, if that's what you mean."

"Thanks for that," I mumbled.

"Hey, Tonto," Joz said, "you know there's a bullet hole in the passenger door of your new car I could put my finger into? You oughta take care of your new toys."

"Who shot at you?" Concern showed in Cassie's voice.

"Someone not familiar with my good and noble side, I suppose."

"Well," Joz said, "it's a silver car. There's one more thing you can fix with duct tape."

Cassie looked at me with an expression I would be pressed to describe, and with more motherly concern than lust.

"You guys weren't arguing when I came in, were you?" Joz said.

"Well, we . . ." It was as far as I got.

" 'Cause with me an' the ol' man, back when we were married, that was usually foreplay."

"We're not you and your ex-husband," Cassie said.

I didn't add that popular opinion held that Joz had bumped off her ex.

Joz turned to me. "Okay, hotshot. Let's talk about the money."

"What money?" I glanced at Cassie. She gave Joz an equally puzzled look.

"There's a manpower war going on here in Austin," Joz said. "We've been able to find that out so far. Landscapers and the maid service people are knocking heads to get the biggest crews, and the fewer of them with green cards, the better. Someone's making money. By the way, you got INS all over the place out there. You didn't know that?"

I turned slowly to Cassie. She looked at a spot on the floor halfway between us. "I thought you came back to help with the vampire business," I said.

"It's all tied together," Joz said. "The money, the green cards, the vampire stuff. Ain't she told you about that yet?"

"I was just getting to that," Cassie said.

The calm breathy notes drop low, then the pace quickens. Each note jams on the heels of the one before, racing and climbing as the saxophone's notes lift into a discordant screech.

CHAPTER EIGHT

Joz sat down on the corner of the desk. Cassie looked at me with one eyebrow raised. That was something I could never do, though I had tried in the mirror a couple of times.

I went around behind the desk, sat in the chair, opened a drawer and took out a glass—an empty jar really, the kind dried beef comes in, as close to fine crystal as my place had to offer.

"Haven't you had enough?" Cassie said.

"Nightcap," I said, poured an inch. I weathered the pursed lips she directed at me.

They waited. Not all that patient, but it was my casa, such as it was. "Mind if I talk while you entertain yourself?" Cassie said. She could have sat on the straight-backed chair, but she leaned her shoulders against the wall.

Joz gave me an unblinking stare.

Cassie said, "There's a place down on First Street where workers, mostly Hispanics, and a few of them illegal, can stand in the morning and work crews can be pick them up for a day of lawn work, painting, whatever. It's survival money, but the INS is all over the area, so some don't even take that risk. We don't know where the illegals willing to work for even less money are being picked up yet, but we will."

"You might try a place down in the outside edge of Southeast Austin, an auto wrecking yard called Eddie Paul's Wrecks." I eyed the tequila I'd poured, didn't really want or need it, realized I had poured it to get up Cassie's sleeve.

"You kidding me about the name?" Cassie said. She thought for a second, added, "How much of this did you already know but didn't share?"

"Didn't get time," I said. "But I have some feel for what's going on. It hasn't gotten as bad as it did that time back in 1990 when that rancher north of L.A. kept those folks in chains at night after they had worked sixteen-hour days."

"He plea-bargained down to corporate racketeering," Cassie said, "got off on the slavery charge."

"Oh." I reached and took a small sip.

"You have any more little surprises you want to share?"

"No."

"Good. Then quit interrupting."

"Sorry," I said, though I wasn't. I splashed down the rest of my libation for punctuation.

Joz pulled the back of one hand across her mouth and stared hard at me.

Cassie's right eyebrow still described an arc, though with its soft yellow hairs on a face as makeup free as hers, it did not have much punch. "We don't mean to imply that you aren't capable of doing a little detecting yourself," she said. "Whoever is getting a grip on the illegals through vampire and satanic superstition is driving them to the crime spree Austin is experiencing. It's also responsible for the scare tactics used by the competition, like your friend Armando."

"He's just a client, and now a former and non-paying one at that."

"Those missing people you were looking for . . ." Cassie said. "Chances are that if you do find them they'll be in the same shape you found Rocio. But remember, these are not people who are natural criminals. They're being driven to it, scared into it."

"And the money?" Joz said.

"It's not the kind of thing you report or pay taxes on," Cassie said. "Somewhere someone is stockpiling a pretty little nest egg of cash from all this."

"It's good to know that you are both motivated by the greater good in this." I stood up. "Now, if you don't mind, I am going to weave my way to the back room. Where are you two staying?"

"Here," Cassie said. I sat back down. "Oh, don't get your shorts tangled into a tighter knot than they already are. We'll be out here in the front room. You'll be safer than you usually are. Bring in the cots, Joz."

With Joz out the door, I said, "Isn't there any crime you should be busting back in that county of yours?"

"Harmon gave me the time off. I asked for it. I really think we can help you on this, and it's fun stuff, not to mention pretty high-profile for a change."

She moved over close. When I looked up at her, she reached and put a soft warm hand on the side of my face. "I know some of this is a little hard for you. I'm sorry for what I said earlier."

The hand felt good, but I moved the rough skin of my face away from it.

She let her hand drop to her side. "I think about you, hope that the very brief time we spent as closer friends than we should have been didn't soften you."

I let out a small puff of breath. "You steamroll me, tell me it's to help me, then you wonder if I might be going soft?" We were back on that again.

"You know what I mean. When we met you had a hardness in you like I rarely see."

"Outside your own family?"

"I mean in a man. Oh, Trav, I'm not saying there isn't a tough side to your life. That's my whole point. You have to be hardy to spend all that quality time with yourself. That can be the easy way to go too. It simplifies things. And for what? How many Christmases have you spent alone? Most of them. What few friends you've had that I know about have hurt you more than your enemies. That's stung, hasn't it? And that just draws you deeper into this hole you call a life, the consuming work, the cactus juice. I wonder if I didn't just screw you up more, when I was trying to open you up then . . . or now." When I did not say anything, she added, "Trav, you've got to learn to trust those around you."

I said, "I'm trying."

"Ya know," Joz said. She came through the door, dropped one rolled cot onto the floor, untied it and began snapping open the wooden legs of the other army cot. "People talk about the passing of what was once the Wild West. But I'll tell you another era that's clicking its heels shut. Marriage. It used to be a simple business arrangement. The man needs free domestic help and someone to squeeze when he's in the mood. For the past half-century more and more women can smell the bad deal in that—or they do once they've tried it. Look at your divorce rates. I'm not makin' this up."

I looked at Cassie. She kept herself busy setting up her cot and didn't look my way.

"So now you got a buncha crabby guys doin' their own socks and sayin' things aren't like they used to be. Well, damned straight."

The record in my mind got stuck on the track of how Joz had divorced herself from all that, in an unpleasant and permanent way for her ex-husband. I said good night, got a curt nod back from both of them. When I headed to the back room I took the bottle with me.

I woke early in the morning to hammering on the door. My head throbbed, but I had had no dreams, which is all I could hope for. I had slept well and undisturbed except for a couple of tiptoed trips to the bathroom by my house guests. The back room is tiny, barely room for a cot pressed against the open bathroom door in a way that does not let it close. There's only a small shower, sink, and toilet in there. Usually it poses no problem for me. As it was, I did not want to see whomever traipsed through the room in their foundation garments, so I kept an army blanket pulled over my head, warm as the little room had gotten.

I shoved my t-shirt into my pants as I went to the door. The cots were gone and so were my guests. I swung the door open without checking first, always a mistake. Borster stood there. The jagged scar that came down from the corner of his mouth in his oily, slightly pockmarked face caught the morning light. It is not a way I wish to be awakened. Beside him stood his walking appendage, Findlay.

The two of them pushed past me and came into my quarters. Both looked around the room, Findlay went to the back and peeked in the door there. "Were you expecting us?" Borster asked.

In my long, and not so lustrous career as a PI there have been few people with whom I have shared as antagonistic a relationship as with Borster. I could not be sure where we had gotten off on the wrong foot, but his missing out on a reward had been at least a couple of two-steps to the left. Perhaps he did not see himself as greedy, merely thought there had been money coming to him that he had earned that had gotten sidetracked. I know I never got any of the money, nor of the pile that came and went in the next revolving door of a case. Somewhere Borster had the idea that I had squirreled away a chunk of the cash. If he only would bother to talk to my landlord or any other creditor, he might get the clear picture. Borster, though—Findlay either, for that matter—did not seem a person to let the facts cloud his judgment.

"Looks like you're still living large," Borster said.

"Are you blind?" I said. I glanced around the room. The place looked neat by default. There was the desk and two chairs in the front room, not even a calendar thumbtacked to the wall. "The car, this suit, and even this desk were gifts in that case you're thinking about. They were given because I wouldn't take the check from at least one of the people who wanted to pay."

"I see clearly enough. I did at the time. I still do." Borster walked close, stood well within my space, his face inches from my own. Findlay moved around behind me. I did not like the feel of this.

"It doesn't really matter," he said. I did not believe him. "That money, or new money. You still owe me large. You see it that way too? What are you working on now?" His oily face leaned even closer.

"I think some other detective is handling that," I said.

"I'm making you my special case."

The door handle turned and opened. Detectives Barnett and Kilgallon stepped into my small crowded office. I felt Findlay move away from behind my back. Borster's head turned slowly to look at them. He stared at them. No emotion showed on his face.

"Morning, Ned," Detective Sergeant Barnett said. "Hope we're not interrupting anything. But we need to question the witness."

"Just a couple of old friends catching up," Borster's voice rasped. He nodded to Findlay. They headed for the door.

Once Findlay and Borster were out of the room I slumped back against the desk.

"What native charm do you exert to so endear you to so many others?" Barnett asked.

"Must be my obvious show of wealth." I looked down at a

hole I noticed in my t-shirt. "You fellows mind if I slip into a shirt?"

"Please do," Kilgallon said. These two were far too polite for my taste. It put me off my expectations of cops, especially after a dose of Borster.

Kilgallon stood in the doorway to the back room while I slipped on my shirt, tie, and shoes. Neither knew me well enough to know that I never carried a gun. Knowing folks like Joz as I did, I may have felt I was somehow evening out the average.

"I take it we're going somewhere," I said. "What's up?"

"You see Watt Stoner yet?" Barnett had come over to stand in the door too. He rubbed a contemplative finger under his lip.

"Yeah. I visited his place once after Lola's death." I had to hope there was no sighting of me at the house yesterday. If they found a latent print or two I had covered myself now. The test would be if they let me go at the end of this conversation.

"We were trying to see him as well. But he gave us the slip."

"He said he'd been moving around a lot." I bent to tie my shoes, listened to them pace around in the front office.

"He won't be now. He's dead."

"Oh." I stood up. "You don't think . . . ?"

"We want to show you something." Barnett's voice came from closer to the doorway.

"I hope you guys didn't get the wrong idea about me living alone."

"Oh, put on your jacket and let's get out of here," Kilgallon snapped. It was the first time that either of them had shown any irritation or anything other than consideration. I welcomed it. The forced good manners of these guys had started to spook me.

We climbed into the car, me in the back.

"You talked with him for quite a while when you did see him, didn't you?"

"Yeah." I shared the gist of my conversation with Watt, left out the part about wondering if Lola was superstitious.

"How did he die?" I asked. The car eased through traffic.

What I wanted to know, but did not ask, Barnett answered for me. "Still waiting for the report. M.E. won't say yet, of course. Looked to me like he died swallowing his own phlegm. Couldn't move his head."

"Was he tied up?"

"Yeah. And all his blood was still in him," Barnett said. That answered my unspoken question about that.

Barnett turned in his seat, looked back at me. "But someone took a cigarette and burned a 'V' into his chest."

I had been mistaken about our heading to police headquarters or any of their other facilities. The cruiser pulled into the parking lot of one of the city's high schools. I'd never been to any of them, but this one seemed to have the standard features—yellow/orange bricks, paved parking lot, tired looking grass where paths didn't crisscross the lawn. The only difference at this site were the half-dozen other police cars and some guys running around in black shirts with large white CRIME SCENE letters across the back.

Uniformed cops were keeping a circle of adults and weeping teenage children back from the yellow tape. I glanced at Barnett and Kilgallon. You could read more in the stone faces on Mount Rushmore than they were sharing.

We pushed through the line of people, who parted. The uniformed cops nodded at the detectives, gave me a glance that wondered if I was a suspect. I began to wonder myself.

We wove through the main string of buildings, walked down along a covered sidewalk until we could pass through to the back, past the climbing bleachers of a stadium. Off to our left stood a barn. We headed toward that.

I could see flashbulbs going off inside. Another photographer was taking a video of the pen areas outside. He swept the camera across a series of the wooden fence—enclosed sections. These were the police cameras. A half-dozen ticked-off-looking media crews huddled near their vans on the far parking lot where they were being kept at bay for the moment by the uniformed police.

As we got closer, I caught the smell. The odor of death. I knew it better than I liked.

Flies buzzed everywhere, in a fierce and annoying manner. The day had only begun to warm up. As it became a scorcher the mess around me would get far worse. We got close enough to see into some of the pens, see the smears of blood.

"Who the hell would do this?" I said.

"That's what those kids back there are asking," Barnett said. "They were raising these as pets and part of a school project."

In the nearest pen a sheep lay twisted on its side. Its throat had been opened by something like a machete. The pool of blood mixed in its white wool and the dirt of the pen had turned dark purple.

To our left a goat had tried to climb the side of its pen. Its front hooves hung over the top. Its head lolled to the side. Entrails strung from its insides all the way back to the center of the pen.

We went from one to the other of the pens. The scenes of carnage filled the barn. Not an animal had been spared. Most had suffered before they had finally died.

"Why are you showing me this?" I asked. We went on to look at the pens outside. The sun was bright enough to make me squint.

They said nothing.

"You guys are homicide cops," I said. "You asked me about Watt Stoner. How does this . . . ?"

"I think," Barnett said, "that's it's time we sat down and had a serious heart-to-heart talk."

MURRAY, Kentucky (AP)—*The mother of a teenager, who police say led a vampire cult linked to two deaths, pleaded guilty to trying to entice a teenage boy into sex as an initiation rite.*

Sondra Gibson, 35, was originally charged with solicitation to commit rape. She instead pleaded guilty to a felony charge of unlawful transaction with a minor. Gibson could have faced five years in prison, but her attorney agreed to five years' probation.

Ms. Gibson is the mother of Rod Ferrell, awaiting trial in Tavares, Florida, on two counts of murder. Police say he led a blood-drinking vampire group involved in the crime.

CHAPTER NINE

Uniformed cops held the growing crowd back, though the line surged in places. The parents looked angrier. The children cried louder. The distant media crews glared our way even harder. Dozens of pairs of eyes watched us as we came back down the walkway, headed for the parked car.

I climbed into the backseat, glad for once to be in an unmarked car. Too many of those in the surly crowd might think the cops had found their perp.

"A gang do that?" I asked, once they were settled and strapped into their seats.

"No." Barnett started the car. He didn't look back at me. "Gangs happen because the collective individuals in them are cowards. If this had been done by a gang it might be a drive-by shooting, maybe some markings on a wall. But most gangs wouldn't have the spine for what happened here."

"Or the stomach," Kilgallon said. He gave me a quick glance.

Barnett wove the car out through the congestion around the school and headed back for downtown Austin. A pickup truck eased into the flow of traffic ahead of us. Four people had crammed into the cab, another eight people with Hispanic faces hunched in the bed of the truck. Each of the passengers stared as we went around them. No one smiled.

"You sure you told us everything you and Watt Stoner talked about?" Kilgallon looked ahead, let the words bounce of the inside of the windshield and back to me. "It'd be interfering with an investigation if you haven't been straight with us."

Now we get to it. I had been expecting the vise grips from these guys sooner.

"Just how much do you know, or think you know?" Kilgallon said.

"Not as much as I should."

"Don't try to be coy." Barnett this time. He sounded tired, and disgusted. "We don't have the time, and it's not your style."

He seemed to know more about my so-called style than I did.

Kilgallon undid his seat belt. He turned slowly all the way around in the passenger seat to stare at me. "You don't see anything from your particular perspective that might be problematic? The police coming to a scene like this to find the media already here, hearing they all got tipped off that all this ties to the vampire story? We had the devil's own time getting them all off a crime scene they'd already mucked up, and footage of this is already on the air at several stations. Think hard. Why does that make everything harder instead of easier for us?"

There had to be a simpler way to say what he had just said. I didn't quibble. "What are you accusing me of?"

"I think you know where we're going with this," Kilgallon said. His voice somehow kept a level pitch and volume.

"Why don't you come right out and say it?"

"Why don't you wipe that beginning of a smug smile off your face?" He stared at me.

"I'm not being smug and I'm damned sure not smiling. Quit fooling around and shoot straight. You think I enjoy waking to see dead animals?"

"All right, guys," Barnett said, his tone that of the parent straightening out the rambunctious kids in the car. He eased the car over to the curb. Traffic was thick around us. We weren't to our destination, wherever that was going to be. He turned in his seat until the two of them faced me over the back of the seat.

"Are you the one who called the media now, and about the holes in Lola's neck, and even about the 'V' burned on Watt Stoner's chest?" Barnett said.

"No. Why would you think that? It's as much a mess for me. I've no reason to want this splashed everywhere. I didn't even know about this until you dragged me here."

"We don't know that you're the blabby type or that you're not. But there's a loose cannon somewhere, and you're as in the middle of being in the know as anyone," Kilgallon added. Their expressions were veiled, though it could have been weariness at dealing with people like me who only distracted them. "We just know that now we're going to have more crazed housewives rushing to the groceries to buy strings of garlic, not to mention the heat we're getting to make all of this stop."

"Dead pets show the serious level to which this has escalated," Barnett said.

"Human bodies don't?" I knew I should have just kept my mouth closed.

Their eyes connected, snapped back to me. No more good cop/good cop anymore. Well, that was something of a relief.

"We figured you'd hear about the pets back there at the school, but you'd find out soon enough. We're trying to find a leak and plug it."

"Well, I'm not it."

"We don't know that. Someone's sure as shit stirring up the press."

"Just be careful. We'll be keeping a closer eye on you," Barnett said. "We track anything to you and you're going to be sorry you ever drifted to this town."

"You telling me to lay off my case?" I said. I didn't want any hysterical media shouting vampire and tromping around, mucking up the trail any more than these two cops did.

"You know we can't do that."

"As much as we'd like to."

"But we can tell you to play your cards close."

"Very close."

"Now, why don't you please get out of the car?"

I stood there, to hell and gone from my office, a good thirty- to forty-block hike away. I did not complain. The sun beat down, hammered at me plodding along in my dark suit. The walk helped maintain my humble and gave me time to think.

I stumbled into my office, looked around. No Cassie. No Joz. No Borster. Good. I peeled off the damp suit, hung it on the straight chair in front of the window. The room felt toasty enough, without air-conditioning, to begin to dry it. In the back I let the rusty shower water trickle across me.

"Did I startle you?" I said.

"No." Sister Consuela's eyes bugged at me. She looked tired, had gathered up a few years and was wearing them since I had seen her last. Her round face had lost some of its farm girl freshness. New lines cut into what had been a smooth forehead.

"You heard that they found Watt Stoner dead, didn't you?"

"It only this afternoon came to me. I am . . . saddened." Her voice came from far down in her throat, a far echo from the usual cheerfulness I expected of her. She had erred to the Pollyanna side in the past. Something had yanked the Norman Vincent Peale right out of her and stomped it flat.

"Know where I was earlier?"

"How could I begin to . . . ?" Her eyes tightened in irritation.

"Driving around, visiting every used bookstore in the city. Did you know we have a ton of them? I struck out too at all of them. Then I thought of you."

"But what . . . ?"

"I had to figure backwards, work with Lola's estimated age. Then I dug to find where she might have gone to school. I was after a class yearbook. They don't keep them at the library, and the new bookstores can't stock them. Then, boom. I thought of you. There's a school here, isn't there? A parochial one. Girls wear the little Catholic girl costumes and all that."

She tilted her head a half inch to the right, but said nothing.

"I had a discussion, or argument with my friend Jimmy Bravuro. We were trying to decide who was more evil. Was it Jeffrey Dahmer, for listening to some inner voice and killing and eating those men he lured to his home? Or was it the company that brought out trading cards of the victims after Dahmer got convicted?"

Sister Consuela lowered her head, in thought or in prayer. She raised it and looked at me, said, "Do scales know lead from gold?"

"Are you going to help me with this or not? Because I've already made the mental connection. I need to get to the physical side. And I will get there, eventually, whether you help or not."

"I always thought you a kindly man," she said, "in spite of your vocation. You cause me to doubt that for the first time."

"You can think of it as fire to fight fire, or however you want. You know the year I want. Well?"

She looked at me, tired, with almost no emotion. Then she showed the sadness I had seen earlier. That tailed into the beginnings of a smile she had to work to achieve. "I'll be right back," she said. She moved down the church hallway like a penguin in high gear.

Somewhere behind Sister Consuela's usually cheerful face there reposed a whole untold story. She kept that as under wraps as a poker player. When she had tottered at the funeral, nearly pitched a faint, she had showed more of her hand than she would have liked. She was part of all this, though, like it or not.

I stood in the hallway near the front door, never invited any further in. She came back in five minutes. Under one arm she carried a mailing envelope. Rubber bands crisscrossed the manila sides.

"You know, don't you," she said, "that he who rides a tiger finds it difficult to dismount?"

"Don't you have any original thoughts?"

"I don't have to. I'm a nun."

She gave me a moment to say something if I wanted. I didn't. I know when the other person holds all the cards. I held out a hand.

"This is just a loan, Travis. Bring it back when you can. We only keep one for each year."

I took the package she held out toward me. I said, "Did you ever notice anything that might have made you think . . . ?"

"The church has a lot of rituals. We had an acolyte once . . ." She froze, looked off at nothing. Her eyes widened. In the hollow at the base of her throat I could see the beat of her heart. It became more rapid. The skin tightened with each thump, thump, thump.

"Go on."

"Nothing. Oh. He called himself Vesago."

"I'm having a hard time . . ."

"Some of them started mixing tomato juice and orange juice. Well, what do you expect when some kids think they've drank the blood of Christ?"

"You're not being . . ."

"There were a few neighborhood pets that were harmed, some maimed. No one was getting the tattoos and piercings then. That came later." Her eyes locked open and stared at something past my left shoulder that I couldn't see when I took a look. "We did have some of the trappings. A cape, a cane. A coffin, some death worship. The worst was . . . was . . ."

"Do you want to sit down? Try this slowly."

"They'd scratch their arms with razors, drink each other's blood. I'd find a row of scratches up one of the girl's arms. They found it all very . . . sexy somehow. You know, I learned a year or so ago that twenty percent of a steak is blood. I don't know why, but it bothered me all of a sudden." She shuddered, stopped speaking.

"Go on." Though I had no clear idea where she would go.

"No. That's all of it. I'm not going to . . . You're the detective. You . . ." She blinked, looked at me. Her eyes came back into focus. "I'm sorry to . . . maybe I shouldn't have . . . Oh. Why don't you go get busy? Do what it is you have to do." Her mouth pursed. She looked ten years older.

"You think I can do it?"

She shook her head, refused to speak. Her lips stayed pursed. Something personal and traumatic was at work here. If I had the money I would have put her in therapy myself. I turned to go, then spun back. She trembled. "Oh, go ahead," I said. "Give me one more."

She hesitated. I started to turn again. She unpursed her lips, said, "It's hard to shave an egg." She tried for a smile, could not quite get there.

I drove to Crystal Canyon Drive, where L. Leroy Hunt's mansion nestled. I have been to streets called Turtle Creek, where there are no turtles and no creek. Years back I had been to Cooper's Pond, where there was no cooper and no pond. Hunt's street had in common with them that there was no crystal and it was not in a canyon. The street did have a lot of bends, sharp turns leading back to cul-de-sacs. His mansion sat back along a twisting street with no outlet. Tax dollars had built the street, but not the fence around the estate.

A gate of black wrought-iron bars stretched across Hunt's driveway between two square pillars of stacked flagstone. I got out of the car. It was a warm day even by Texas spring standards. Heat slapped into me, making my shirt stick to me. The eye of a camera lens high on the fence looked down at me, swung with me as I walked. There was a pearl button in a brass ring beside the gate, a small light over it, lit even though the sky was a mid-day pale sheet of aluminum cloud mass above me.

I reached for the button. Before my thumb got to it, a scratch-ing rasp came from the speaker beside the button, then a voice. "Go away."

The reception at Madam Rostini's place was, well, more recep-tive. At least the door opened for me when I knocked at her cottage.

"Don't say it," I said. "You knew I'd be back."

"Get in here," Eva said. She still wore black, though a differ-ent outfit than she had worn at the cemetery.

"Afraid the neighbors will see me?"

"I fear for your life, stupid."

She closed the door, turned to me and put her back against it.

I moved to the center table but did not sit down. I turned to face her. "You mind my asking one trick-of-the-trade question?"

Her head tilted down and to the right. She looked at me from that angle and waited.

I said, "What single gimmick do you find works best in the fortune-telling game?"

"What scam, you mean?"

"Whatever."

I didn't expect her to answer, but she did. "That everyone

has some dark and dirty little pile of laundry in their past that makes their own hair rise, whether it's a person, something done or not done, or just their own ruined expectations. Now you."

"What?"

"Now you have to share something."

"Like . . . ?"

"What little trick-of-the-trade works best for you in the detection scam?"

I hesitated. "Oh, what the hell," I said. "Suspect everyone."

Her head tilted back as she laughed.

"Where's the pizza man? Doesn't he get frequent caller points?"

"Please. Don't say the word. It's been celery and carrots all day."

"Why?"

"What brought you here? And don't tell me I should already know. I want to hear you say it."

"You tried to trip me at the cemetery. Why?"

"I thought you . . . were after someone else." Her big eyes looked up at me. One hand lifted to pat the coins that hung around her neck into place. The other slipped behind her, turned the lock on the door.

"You're mad at him. But you don't want me to talk with him. Why's that?"

"What makes you think I'm mad at anyone?" she said.

"Just something I detected. It's what I do. Remember?"

"Who do you think you're talking about?" Her eyes confirmed her fear that I did know.

"Your brother?"

Her mouth opened. She slowly forced it closed.

I held up the package I had gotten from Sister Consuela. I had taken the rubber bands off and tucked them into one of my

121

suit jacket pockets. I slid out the yearbook. "Why didn't you tell me up front that you and Lola were in the same class at school, that your brother, Levi, was a year ahead of the two of you? I understand he was an acolyte once."

Her face flushed to the roots of her red hair. She was a pretty, even a beautiful woman. But I would never dare tell her that, for several reasons. One is that, when a woman is sensitive about her weight, as she seemed to be, it is always dangerous to say she is pretty. She thinks you are calling attention away from her weight. It was a no-win situation, and I did not go there.

She let out a lungful of air, seemed to diminish. "Maybe we should sit down," she said. She flicked off the light to the sign outside that advertised her fortune-telling business.

"You must be feeling flush to turn away business."

"I had the impression you wanted to talk," she said. She moved closer. "So talk."

I moved to the table, pulled out a chair. "Tell me about the cult." I sat down.

She held the other chair, reeled a half step back. "How much did . . . Sister Consuela tell you?"

"Let's pretend she told me nothing. Fill me in from the beginning."

"No."

"I understand you wanting to protect your brother. You use a different last name now, not Damocles like you both had then. Any reason?"

"You waste your time. I will . . . *can* say nothing." She sat down in the other chair. Not a plop as I have seen some people do who fancy they are heavy. But light and delicate as a leaf falling onto a pool of water.

"You think he won't harm you, that the family ties will protect you. If it gets dicey, they won't. That's one of the most common mistakes. The bulk of all violence in this country is domestic.

Lots of people make that mistake."

"That's husband and wife, not . . ."

"Blood is thicker than water. Is that where you're headed? Save your breath. Whoever is behind this is killing the people who knew Lola well, ones who she talked with. I'm not saying your brother Levi is the one. I'm not that far yet. Why don't you just tell me how it all got started with Lola and Levi? Focus on that. I'll find out anyway."

"I imagine you will. Why don't you go and do that?"

"Because you know as much as anyone. It's okay to hold out on me. I'm just some private guy trying to do some good. But you hold out on the detectives investigating this and they will get out the tongs and bamboo splints."

"I knew it would be you. You don't seem to . . . nothing can . . . Oh, why don't you just . . . ?" I was starting to get used to people not making a great deal of sense.

"Whatever's been going on is about to be public soon. Have you been catching the news? The town's in vampire hysteria. I'm not saying there will be pitchforks and torches, but the villagers are stirred up. Do you have a pentagram tattoo somewhere on you as well?"

"Think you'd like to take a look?" There it was again, a bit of that coquettish smile, snapped away as quickly though as a wisp of smoke in the breeze from a fan.

"Start at the beginning. You're all back in school. What was going on? How did it get started?"

"You could check with our parents."

"You know I'd have looked there. They're both dead. Quit trying to be the good sister. I doubt he's even called or visited you in the past few years. He lives in a mansion. You live like this." I looked around at the inside of her cottage, wondered where I got off talking like that. It was better than where I lived.

Her face had a firm set. I had gotten all the way to her stone wall, was going to get no further. "Maybe you can tell me this," I said. "What's a doppelganger?"

Her pale face got a shade whiter. "Why do you . . . ?"

"Lila," I said. "What's that all about?"

Eva sighed, some of the resistance easing out of her. "Her name isn't Lila. It's Liriel Hanlon, and that may not even be her *real* name. He found her someplace."

"Levi?"

"Who do you think?"

"What was she supposed to do, scare Lola somehow? Bring her under Levi's control? How? For what?"

She wanted to speak, and not speak. She struggled with it.

"It's all going to lead to him. Help me understand it. That's all I ask. If anyone is disposed to be understanding it's me, not the police. You won't get this much courtesy from them."

She held her breath for a moment, then let it out in a long sigh. "Oh, what the hell."

I waited.

"It was all a game at first. Silly stuff. You know how kids are."

"You tell me."

"This was a long time ago, way before Stephen King."

"But kids always like ghost stories, scary things."

She suppressed a shudder, looked away from me, but talked. "Levi was a dominant kid, obsessed with succeeding. He was a control freak, call it what you will. I was his first sucker. Then he roped my best friend Lola in."

"You sucked each other's blood, played that game?"

She nodded slowly.

"Anybody ever get hurt?"

"No. Well, nothing permanent."

"The pets? The maimed ones?"

"That was . . . one of the things . . . when I decided to get out."

"So this hasn't been going on since then?"

"No. Lola and I broke away some time ago, years ago. But . . ." She stopped herself.

"You think Lola went back?"

She nodded. Her eyes glistened, but she held back any tears if she had been headed that way.

"Why?"

"Lola craved success. I mean *really* craved it."

"She *was* successful."

"I mean big success. Real success. Name in the lights, all that. Not just being good in some backstreet pub."

"And that business about Lila. How was a doppelganger, or whatever, supposed to affect Lola?"

"Like I said. Levi found her somewhere. She looked like Lola, or almost. Even more so after a make-over."

"What do you think happened?"

"I think . . . I think . . . Lola was . . . you have to remember, pretty strung out, wired, ready to try anything."

"And?"

"She might've been convinced she was able to sell her soul to the devil."

"Are you serious?"

"More than you could know."

"You believe that some dark-side twin can steal a person's soul?"

"It doesn't matter what I believe," she said. Her red curls shook back and forth with the head shake. "But it could have easily unnerved Lola."

"She was an adult, a little snappy and quick on the draw lately from what I hear, but nobody's fool."

"She had become bitchy. And what was making her that way was her decision. It had been a bad one. Even worse. It wasn't getting her where she wanted to go fast enough."

"Levi was just stringing her along?"

"You know, Levi really believes he *is* the devil. He can be very convincing. She had gotten pretty strung out from working too hard. Maybe she believed him."

"Aren't there times you really believe you can see the future?"

"You know that that's not *all* a scam. I sense more than the average bear. People lay down more clues than they think, body language, the way they dress, talk."

"I'm an open book, eh?"

"I can tell a lot about you. You're a chronic loner, scared of feeling anything too deeply. Anyone ever told you that before?"

"It comes up," I said.

BATON ROUGE, Louisiana (AP)—*Four teenagers believed to be part of a self-described "vampire cult" were returned to Florida to face charges of killing the parents of one of the suspects.*

Police say the youths drank their own blood and that of mutilated animals and became attracted to vampires because of a best-selling role-playing game. Defense lawyers called them scared youths and dismissed the vampire claims.

CHAPTER TEN

Jimmy Bravuro sat across the table from me. He winced at a high note that wavered, then broke. Lila stood in the center of the stage. She wore the same kind of blue dress I had seen on Lola, and the lights were doing all they could. It was not enough, would never be enough.

People at the tables murmured as she sang, wondered out loud how someone could look so much like another person and sound so little like her.

Lila finished the song. Halfhearted applause rippled through the crowd, some of it because she had stopped. She set the bar for bad, maybe the worst I had ever heard. She had the words right and looked great, but her singing was a new low for me. I saw Owen hustle past the end of the bar toward the back. He saw me, but kept moving. He threw both arms upward in a helpless gesture as he disappeared into the back.

Jimmy clapped his hands a couple of polite times, leaned closer to me. Lila stepped away from the mike, headed toward her dressing room to take a break. The chatter at other tables around us picked up. "You're looking like you were shot out of the wrong end of the cannon. You been working too hard?"

"Is it hard to make it in the music biz in this town, Jimmy?"

"Hard? It's impossible." He wore a ball cap, black t-shirt, jeans, and boots. "It's my night off," he had said when I asked him earlier. But I had never seen him wear anything fancier on stage.

"*You've* made it," I said.

"If six CDs and an average of two gigs a week is making it, then I have. But I don't want to tell you how many years I put in, and still the only troubles I *don't* have are income tax ones, 'cause you gotta have an income first."

While I was still working up a snappy response to that, Up-and-Down Jonesy came out of the back and wove through the tables over to ours.

"Jimmy, you old dog you!" He sure sounded full of enthusiasm, an exuberance that contrasted with our mood after listening to Lila. He wore a white peasant blouse, black slacks, and black lizard-skin cowboy boots. His head of thick brown hair swept back and fell to the top of his collar, making him look more than a little like Robin Hood. The shirt helped that more than hurt.

"Darrell," Jimmy said back with an enthusiasm that sought to echo Jonesy's but came off flat.

"Sit down," I said. "I've been wanting to talk to you."

"Oh, you're the guy Jeezy hired. The Indian."

"What's Owen do, put out a newsletter?"

Jonesy pulled out a chair, sat. "What do you think, Jimmy?" He leaned closer. "Is she as bad as I think she is?"

Jimmy shrugged. "I don't know. I've heard worse. What'd you think?" He said it to me, but Jonesy answered.

"Oink." Jonesy made a wrinkled-nose face that matched his comment. As it left his relaxed face, inner delight lit up his features, made him look younger than I'd seen him look in a spell.

"Yet you seem to enjoy her singing somehow," Jimmy said.

"Sure makes *me* look good."

Life is a sure enough study in contrasts and comparisons. Jimmy's eyes swept the crowd. A couple in suit and evening dress sat next to two jeans-clad women who had not heard the

'60s were over. "I hear you've shifted over to the prime sets. Doing the ten o'clock show, eh?"

"I have." Jonesy shared a wide smile. "And did you hear I got a new CD offer?"

"No kidding?"

"This could be big. Some recording studio guys who stopped in at the club noticed me."

Jimmy's narrowed eyes swept across me and the rest of the crowd. He landed back on Jonesy, turned on a smile for him. "Well, I've always been a silver-lining sort of guy. I hate to think about what happened to Lola. But I'm glad to hear you came out of it well."

"You know how it is," Jonesy's voice was at once humble again. "We all work hard and pay our dues. Sometimes one of us gets a break."

"Have you any ideas about Lola?" I said.

"I've been through all that with the police."

"Don't you want to help?" I watched his face.

"What kind of ideas?"

"Like who would kill her?" Jimmy said. He could see where I was going.

Jonesy shrugged. "The only part of her life I know anything about was from in here, the customers and some of the men she saw."

"You know her ex-husband was killed, don't you?"

"Yeah. Damned shame. He was about the best of the lot." He shifted in his chair.

"Do you think she was hungry enough for fame to do something rash, to take extreme risks?"

"Hungry? She was a piranha."

"Hate to say it," Jimmy said, "but ambition drives a lot of those who make it in this biz. Do you think the late easygoing Don Walser would have made it if he hadn't been willing to do two gigs a day, seven days a week? He could sing and yodel with the best of them, but that wasn't going to get him anywhere without exposure."

"Hey," Jonesy said, "what's become of Dutch Hitchcock? I don't see him around anymore."

"Haven't you heard? He picked up and moved the hell and gone down to Terlingua, Texas. He's guiding raft trips on the Rio Grande and singing at the campfires at night."

"I thought he was a flatlander, from out around Lubbock."

"He used to have a shop next to my office on Brazos Street," I said. "It was called 'Lubbock or Leave It.' It looks like he left it."

"I hear he's writing better songs than ever," Jimmy added. "Down there in the shadows of the Chisos Mountains and Big Bend National Park. There's inspiration in such places."

"And heat," Jonesy said. "It can be a real blister down there during summer and fall."

"All that part of Texas needs is a little water, breeze, and cool evenings to be a paradise."

Jonesy said, "That's all hell needs."

"Well, be that as it may, that's where Dutch went."

"Yeah, but how could he leave his public behind?" Jonesy looked back and forth at each of us. "You've got to be careful about your momentum in this biz. It's everything. Once I started on the downside I didn't think I'd ever be able to dust myself off, get started again. But I have better material, fresh songs— and you know how those are like your children. It was a bit of luck that recording crew coming around. I'm sorry Lola is no longer alive. But she did me a huge favor. They probably came to hear her, not me. Too bad she isn't around for me to thank her."

I thought that Jimmy showed considerable restraint in not mentioning that working in a dive like Owen's place was hardly having a public.

"Luck's a big part of this business," Jimmy said. "I'll grant you that."

Jonesy still seemed as wound up as a dime-store watch. "The breakthrough for me came in knowing that the songs, if they are to work, need to be ones I enjoy singing and resinging, ones I can listen to on tape and be entertained by myself. They need the content and character for that. I tell you, I have a handful of songs like that now, and it's like having children who are doing well in school."

Jimmy turned to me. "What's up with you? You've been as quiet as a handful of clams."

I like being left on the outside of a conversation as well as the next guy. I had been half listening and half watching the audience. This is indeed a strange business. On any night in Austin you can go to anywhere from thirty to fifty clubs and hear live musicians, and very talented ones. While all that is good for the public, it does add a two-edged sword to the musician's life. Some very good singers, like Lola, end up working in places like this one just to get by.

I felt Owen's presence, looked up. He hovered by our table. His glance swept to the empty stage. Lila was still between sets. "Whaddya think?"

Jimmy looked away. I could not recall him ever saying a harsh word against another person. But he could dodge a direct question with the best of them.

Owen looked at me.

"I'm no expert," I said, "but if the glass in front of me held milk it would be cottage cheese by now."

"I know. She's no Lola. There's no getting around that. I just hope some of the crowd's left by the time you get on stage, Darrell."

"We'll see," Jonesy said. He did not look too concerned. He

turned his head to Jimmy.

Jimmy glanced at his wrist where he wore no watch. "I've got to shake a leg. You still going to stay on the trail, Trav?"

Before I could answer, Owen interrupted, "Should you find the guy, Trav, you don't gotta do nothin'. Just tell me who it is. Then step outta the way. You let me take over. Hear?"

The long tiled hallways were quiet and felt clammy—hard to tell how much of that I had brought with me. I did not enjoy coming to the morgue after midnight. The click of my steps echoed the length of the building. I came to the swinging metal doors with small square windows, pushed one side open and went inside.

Vito stood bent over the stainless steel table. He wore a white lab coat and stood with his back turned toward me. I could see the flesh color of a corpse stretched out in front of him. There was no need to go closer. He used a hand-held saw with a round blade on the end of a power drill to cut open the skull. There was something about the sound of that blade whirling through bone that made the hairs on my nape stand out.

I made no noise, but after a moment Vito let the saw wind down. He turned around, looked at me. Blood spattered the front of a plastic lab apron and his rubber gloves. A fleck or two had landed on one lens of his glasses and on the square cloth mask that covered his mouth and nose. He put down the saw, tugged off a glove and moved the mask down under his chin.

He said, "What brings you down here at this time of night? Nothing new has come in that should interest you. Don't you have a social life? Are you just lonely?"

I had interrupted Vito in one of his being alone times. He could be a little snappish. He had a habit of thrusting his chin forward when he was hurried or crowded. It pushed out like the bow of a ship now.

He tugged off the other glove, tossed the pair of them into a bin. He went over to elbow the faucet of a deep steel sink and wash his hands.

"What's your wife think about these hours?"

"My wife is delighted that I have a job."

"I hope she *sounds* more delighted than you do when you say that word."

He let out a small puff of air.

"You're the one who started all this," I said. I went over to stand against the wall, leaned on it since there were no chairs in Vito's little arena.

"Want to see something that sums it all up?"

"What?"

He finished washing his hands, dried them. A rolling table of surgical tools had been pushed close to the steel table with the corpse I had not yet looked at. Vito picked up a long-handled pair of forceps. He poked around in the trash barrel where he had just tossed the soiled gloves. His arm raised and he held a t-shirt he had had to cut off the victim, or whoever it was on the table. "Look at this," he said, held the other corner of the t-shirt out so I could read it.

Across the front, it read, "I'm with stupid." An arrow pointed up from the words. "He was wearing this when he tried to make a dash across I-35 at night. He dropped the t-shirt back into the trash. "And they want to know what killed him."

"That can't be homicide," I said.

"Not unless someone chased him out there, some gangbanger who was going to pop a cap on him anyway."

"You're in a mood," I said.

"Long day." Vito waved an arm, turned and walked. I followed him past a wall of doors that held bodies on trays behind the small square metal doors. He went into his office. His toe hooked the wooden swivel chair on wheels. He spun it and dropped into it. The springs squeaked a complaint. I eased into a straight-backed chair by the door.

Vito reached to pull one of the desk drawers open. He rummaged around until he found half a pack of crumpled cigarettes. They were unfiltered, Camels, if I saw the rumpled label right.

I watched him twist the end of one. The tobacco was too dry and was falling out. He lit it and the end flamed for a second. "I thought you quit."

He squinted past the twin clouds he snorted out his nose. "Have you tracked down our Béla Lugosi yet? Please say you have so I can shake off forty reporters a minute during daylight hours."

"You think there really *is* a vampire?"

Vito gave an elaborate shrug, but his jaw was tucked back in where it belonged. "If you listen to any television station in town, yes. Myself, I have doubts. There could just be a lot of coincidence, a damned lot." He held the cigarette out to look at it, surprised it had burned down nearly to his fingers. "It's not so much what's really happening anyway. It's the pall of a certain kind of fear that is being cast. You can bet it's there to hide something far more serious than you can see or imagine."

"Why me?" I asked. "Why did you turn me onto this in the first place?"

"Oh, don't shovel me a load of crap," he snapped. "You know you crave obstacles, suffering, intensity. It's as much a part of you, Travis, as it was of Don Quixote to joust with windmills."

"Is that a nice way of saying I'm a sucker?"

"Let's just say you are the kind of a guy who gets things done . . . in spite of obstacles."

"You think there are going to be people who try to stop me, some of them high-ranked people?"

Vito waved away my question along with a cloud of smoke he swept with one hand.

He put the cigarette out, took longer to do it than he needed. He looked up at me, squinting as he tilted back in his chair. "It's a compliment, Travis. You should take it that way. I'm betting that all you have to show for your efforts so far are a bunch of dead ends, people who either won't talk to you or who lie like seventeen rugs. You've probably got no better idea of what's going on now than when you started, or if you have an idea it's so half-baked and such a long shot that you don't even dare talk about it."

I neither shook my head nor nodded. I leaned back in my chair, almost tilted over until I caught myself.

"This is where any reasonable person would back out, throw their hands up, cry *basta*. But not you. I'll bet it's having so little, being given nothing concrete that's just the red flag in front of the bull to you."

"I hope this isn't headed toward some Sitting Bull joke."

"I might say you're bull-headed, but otherwise my intent stops there. You know that I have almost no sense of humor." He fiddled with the pack of cigarettes, took out another and tamped it down until it looked two-thirds the length of a normal cigarette. He pinched the ends, then lit it, seemed to smirk past the new cloud.

"You're not doing much toward building my confidence about solving this."

"What do you think's going on so far?"

"If I was pressed for time to make a sketch, with no consequences involved, I'd say that Lola was in a tangle with a couple of high school acquaintances who were amateur Satanists, Levi and Eva Damocles. A woman named Lila fits into the whole mess, a woman Levi brought around to mess with Lola's head. Superstitious Hispanic hard-working illegal aliens are tangled up somehow. Lola may have known something, or not. She paid back some stolen money to the church she once attended, then she was killed with the evidence aimed at a vampire. Does that sound enough like late-night television for you?"

"It's okay as a hypothesis. But what's the motivation? And there's a flaw or two."

"Such as?"

"Let's say this Levi, or Eva, is the person behind Lola's death. Doesn't it seem like they wouldn't be pointing the evidence toward themselves? And why kill a handful of other people in the same way? What's to be gained from that?

I sighed. "You're right. I don't really have a hell of a lot. And I'm tired, don't know when I've been so tired."

"Haven't lost any blood without knowing it, have you?" Vito lowered himself in his seat until he was level and staring at me. "What is it brings you to the morgue of all places? You're just lonely, aren't you? You just needed to be around some friend, didn't you?"

I looked around the room, out the door to the wall of drawers holding bodies. I was not too anxious to have Joz or Cassie show up at my office again, nor Borster. "You've got a room here somewhere where you crash sometimes, don't you? You think the corpses would mind if I bunked here for the night?"

Vito reached and tugged a sleeping bag out from under the desk. "Use this if you like. I might as well go see that wife of which you so cavalierly speak. I'll have to lock up when I leave. But I'll be back at 6 A.M. if that's all right."

"Suits me."

"Just don't keep the others up with your singing or anything," Vito said. The ghost of a smile flickered across his tired face. He got up and left me there to sleep with the dead.

The lights on the Fortune-Telling sign snapped off. An hour later, the lights inside the house went out. The white cottage was nestled in the shadows of towering live oak trees. Soft steps moved across the grass. A hand reached and tried the lock of the front door. Locked. The window too. The steps went back to the door. There was a soft scratching of metal on metal.

A cruising patrol car came down the street from the left, kept going. From the other direction came a man walking a golden retriever on a leash.

The soft steps moved away from the cottage into the shadows, kept going. There would be another time.

Few people seem to care much about knowing what the future holds early in the morning. But she was used to getting up early. Today was no exception.

She opened the front door in her robe, looked each way to make sure no one was on the street. She reached and grabbed for the paper. A gust of wind snapped the door shut behind her. She would not have seen the thin scratch lines around the lock if it had not. What the hell? *In a pinch before she had opened the damn thing with a credit card, but she would add another deadbolt lock.*

CHAPTER ELEVEN

The building where L. Leroy Hunt had his offices is square in the heart of downtown corporate Austin. A huge pink granite tower with mirrored glass windows rose shoulder-to-shoulder with the other high-rise buildings.

An information and security kiosk sat in the middle of the wide lobby, centered in the wide black tiles of the floor. I went wide around it while the lone man in uniform spoke with what looked like a salesman asking for directions.

The elevator doors opened and I hurried toward them, took a step back when Detectives Barnett and Kilgallon stepped out.

"Well, well, well," Barnett said. He wore a gray suit today, light blue shirt behind the tie. He had missed a spot while shaving, leaving a black stubble patch under his right cheek. It made him seem almost human.

Kilgallon looked up and down at my suit. "You look like you slept in that. Were you drunk last night?"

"I didn't try to take my pants off over my head or anything," I said. "If that's what you mean." The two of them stood in my path to the elevator, made no move to step aside.

"Here to bother Hunt?" Barnett asked. "Well, good luck. *He's* in a mood. What do you know about him so far?"

"Just what Owen told me. That Hunt is left-handed and keeps his change in his right pocket."

"Big tipper at the club, eh?" Kilgallon pulled a pad out of his inside suit coat pocket. "You might be barking up the wrong tree here." He looked at a page he opened. "This man has alibis the way my Aunt Gertie has piles."

"Your Aunt Gertie's problem aside, I still need to ask him a question or two."

"Don't say we didn't warn you." Kilgallon put his notebook away. The two turned in unison, moved around me, and clicked across the lobby.

The long elevator ride up to Hunt's floor gave me time to collect my thoughts and listen to some snappy shopping music.

The receptionist up on Hunt's floor sat behind a desk big enough for small planes to land on and take off again. She looked up at me like she knew she was very important, and I was not.

"I'd like to see Leroy Hunt," I said.

She suppressed a malicious grin, almost laughed out loud.

Before she could share any of her biting cynicism with me, I added, "Tell him I'm off to see his wife's lawyer about Lola next."

"They're getting a divorce," the receptionist snapped. She seemed immediately sorry she had been lured into talking at all.

"Exactly, and the lawyer would love to get anything juicy he could use to pry more money out of Hunt."

Doubt flitted in a heat-lightning shadow across her face. She reached for the phone. Five minutes later, she ushered me to Hunt's office. The receptionist refused to look directly at me during any moment of the hike down the hall.

She stood outside Hunt's door, waved me in. Now she gave me a look like it was time for me to get mine. The thought seemed to be very satisfying to her.

Hunt sat behind his desk trying to look busy. But it is hard to rustle around a single sheet of paper more than once and still look like you know what you are doing. I had looked into what Hunt's company did—bought up other people's mortgages, as I understood it, and put the squeeze on whoever needed squeezing. I gathered from his success that he was good at it.

He slammed the paper down and began to shout at me before I had gotten halfway across the room. "What's this load of cow flop about telling my wife's lawyer something? I don't even know you. What is it you think you have on me?"

He wore a charcoal suit with a hint of a pinstripe. Stark white shirt with a red tie. His face was only halfway to the brightness of the tie. But at the current rate it would get redder.

It was a big room. It took me a while to get all the way across it.

"We met briefly once," I said. "It was in Lola's dressing room. You've been an obvious and frequent patron of Owen Peasey's club."

"That and a dollar won't even get you on the subway in New York these days. If you have a point make it quickly, then get out." He had a small square face, eyes that could glare with the best of ferrets.

"I think you misunderstand why I'm here." I stopped when I was across the desk from him. He didn't suggest that I sit. "That business about your wife's lawyer was just to get past the overzealous keeper of the gate out there."

"I don't give much of a rat's bushy behind. You think you know something. Spill it. Or I'll have the guards toss you out of here. Better yet, I'll do it myself." He half rose from his seat.

I walked slowly closer, bent across the top of his desk, so he could have a good clear shot. "There's a short rap sheet on you," I said. "Domestic violence. You're a wife beater. But I doubt if you ever threw a punch at a man."

I thrust my chin forward, a little trick I had gotten from Vito.

His fists clenched, unclenched. I thought of the bruises on Lola's arms. Though I had no proof that he had put them there, it was not too hard to imagine that he had. I hoped he would try something. This was a contest. He made me think of the late chess player Bobby Fischer's comment that, "I like the moment when I break a man's ego." Hunt was competitive, and I was in his milieu. I lowered my chances of getting much out of him.

He looked at me, not a glare, but its second cousin. "You come in here, invade my privacy and my workday with something that amounts to little more than a fishing trip, or witch hunt. And you speak abusively. If you had done even a smattering of checking around about me . . ."

The two chairs on the other side of his desk were red leather and looked very comfortable. He had still not invited me to sit, nor did it look like he was going to.

I said, "I know your best friend is City Councilman Jake Hunger, a politician a little to the right of Rush Limbaugh. If that's where the veiled threat is headed. You've helped him with a lot of investments here in Austin. He owns a chunk of that methadone clinic near the Devil's Due. I found that out when I worked out the puzzle of why the neighborhood was getting special patrol car treatment from the men in uniform. Is that how you found Lola, by stopping in at the Devil's Due for a beverage after setting up that investment for him?"

He started to rise from his chair, stopped himself, lowered back into the power spot. From my poking around I knew I had gotten closer to the truth than he liked. He ground about half an inch off his molars without saying anything. When he did speak, it was as simple as a string of pearls on a black dress. "Get out."

"You do realize that I'm not here to hurt you, but to protect you. You're the next logical victim. Whatever Lola told you, however innocent it may have seemed, might make it worth killing you."

He took a long breath, leaned back in his chair and looked at me. "Why do you presume I need protecting?"

"It's just that other people who had that kind of inside information from Lola may be in trouble, could be viewed as some kind of threat."

"By whom?"

"I'm still working on that part. But Watt Stoner is dead."

"Watt was a weak man. He wasn't going to last long anyhow."

Hunt rubbed a forefinger and curled hand under his nose in the manner of a prizefighter stepping into the ring. I wondered if he practiced these little manly gestures.

"Lola never mentioned anything she was involved in that might pose a threat?"

"I'll tell you what I told a couple of flatfeet who left this office not too much before you are going to leave it. Lola talked about a lot of wacky things. But I never listened. I wasn't around her for her conversation." He gave me a locker-room grin, one man-of-the-world to another.

He sat and stared, as still as you can get without someone trying to perform CPR on you. I gathered that the interview was over. I turned and started for the door.

His voice stopped me, "You really think I have anything to worry about?"

I looked back over my shoulder. "I figure the only reason you're alive so far is because someone couldn't crack the security at your home right away. But give them time."

He didn't say anything.

"If that's what they want, they'll do it," I said.

His hands fell flat on the desk and he looked away from me. He hid whatever flickered on his face. As I went out his door, I liked to think he was dealing with fear, even a little self-loathing.

The sun eased toward the horizon and someone came out of Eva's place as I pulled up by the Madam Rostini sign. The lady leaving looked like someone who had been told a piece of good news.

I knocked and entered. Eva looked up from the tarot cards she had placed into a box.

I said, "I thought you read the future in crystal balls."

"I'm sure you didn't come here to talk about crystal balls. What brings you out on an otherwise nice night?" She wore a black skirt and a white blouse. The string of gold coins around her neck made a pleasant clatter as she tossed her head.

"I had such an invigorating chat with Leroy Hunt today that I thought I would top it off with a chat with you."

As a feeler, it fell flat. Eva looked across the table at me with those big eyes of hers. "You do know Hunt, don't you?" I said. "Didn't Lola mention him?"

She tilted her head, the soft red hair fell to that side, her eyes peered back at me from the new angle. As coy goes, Eva could be first-string varsity when she set her mind to it. I glanced around the room looking for a fresh topic of conversation.

A bowl of fruit—apples, bananas, oranges, even a pineapple— sat on the table where the crystal ball usually rested. "Can you tell the future with that?"

"No, silly. That's part of my diet. What makes you think I want to see the future in everything?"

"Diet?" I said.

"Girl stuff, you know. I'm not admitting that I have always liked food better than sex, but the mirror in my house *is* over the dining area."

I took a half step back toward the door.

"That was a joke," she said, laughing for me. "Why don't you sit down? You could tell me why you're here. I don't make you nervous, do I?" She said it like she hoped she did.

"I came here to see if you could get me in to see your brother."

"What a disappointment. You bring me candy, you bring me

flowers, and now you want to talk about my brother."

"What are you talking about?"

"Oh, just tinking around with your head. Why would I take you there?"

"Look, all I want to do is clear up a few things. If Levi's clean, you have nothing to fear. I thought you were a little miffed with him, at least that's the way I read how you behaved at Lola's funeral."

"He's my brother."

"I tumbled to that already. Are you afraid of implicating him somehow?"

"I'll tell you a story." She leaned back in her chair. Her pretty face twisted into more of a knot than I would have liked. "A kid is looking around all over the street one night when a cop comes up to him. 'What're you looking for?' the cop says. The boy says, 'I lost a dollar.' The cop helps him hunt a while, then says, 'You sure you lost it around here?' The boys says, 'No. It was down about a block that way.' The cop says, 'Then why're you looking here?' The boy says, 'Because the light's better.' "

"If you think I'm looking in the wrong place, then what can it hurt?"

"Why don't we stay here and . . . talk. Levi's having some kind of little party tonight, and I'm sure we'd just be in the way."

"Think of it as a chance to dress up real nice and show off," I said.

"What makes you think Levi has anything to do with anything? What grounds do you have?"

"For one, the fact that you haven't been hurt or threatened yet kind of points to him."

Something flittered across her face. Whatever it was, she did not share it.

"Stay here," she said, pushing herself to her feet. "I'll get myself together."

Faraway a single dog began to bark, then howl—each note stretching into long, wolf-like notes of anguish.

Soon another dog took up the note. Then dogs began to howl for blocks, spreading through the city like a grass fire.

"Dogs howling?" the 911 operator said into her headset.

"Do something."

"What?"

"You telling me I should call someone who cares?"

Other lines were ringing. The operator's hand moved forward to make the switch. "Your words, sir. But feel free to go with them."

CHAPTER TWELVE

A full moon shone bone-white bright when not tangled up in wispy clouds in the black sky. When it popped clear it stood out stark against the night. The wind blew like a cool knife whetting itself. I looked up at it past the dead limb of a tree and the metal points of the black wrought-iron fence that surrounded the grounds.

I closed my door, said to Eva, who got out of the other side, "I don't mind telling you that there have been moments in the past where I have sat in theaters saying to myself, 'It's only a movie.' "

She looked up at the sky that framed the gothic lines of the house. "You gotta remember that I grew up with a brother who wished every day was Halloween. Tonight's a beautiful night to him."

An irritating wind slapped us around as we moved past all the other parked cars and hurried up the flagstone walk that led to the front door. The wind yanked at my jacket and tugged my hair out in a straight line. I should have been glad that it no longer rained, but this kind of wind can set in for ten days straight in Austin and have the calmest person ready to go out and commit an ax murder. Combine that with a full moon when the usual crazies are itching for blood and you have conditions I do not crave.

Eva's pale white finger pressed the onyx button at the door. We heard no chimes, but a minute or two later the door clicked open and swung wide like the opening of a bank vault. A tall man, six-five or so and in a black suit and black shirt, opened the door.

" 'Lo Ebbie," Eva greeted him. "We're here to see Levi. Is he around?"

"He is visible." The man had a bass voice that belied the young lines of his face. He looked at me as if I was something he had scraped off the bottom of his shoe, then waved us inside.

We clicked down a long hallway, heard the music grow louder as we neared the flickering light of a room off to one side. I recognized Lola's voice in the recording as we entered the room, but this was not any song I had heard her sing. The speakers were hidden all around the room. The songs coming from them seemed haunting. What made them so was a voice that spoke between each song. Her recorded voice would say, "Lola Pillac-cherosi," and gave a date. The voice of the dead woman. That was the part that tugged at the hairs on the back of my neck. Then she would begin singing the next song, and what songs they were. These made any of the torch songs she sang in the past seem child's play. These must have been her own lyrics, her own torment. The dates she gave were only a month or two back, different before each song. She must have written them recently. There was no hiding the quality of Lola's voice and the emotional intensity which she invested in all of her singing.

> Each twist of the ladder finds you down one more
> rung,
> Caught in the echoes of songs yet unsung,
> Long since you were promised a home in the stars
> Dim flickers of light seen through smoke in the bars.
>
> They pushed and they pulled, until centered on path,
> You were left all alone to work out the math;

Every friend you once thought had your interest at heart
Cannot see or hear you, you stand so apart.

Eva gave my arm a tug. I realized I stood in place, listening like the RCA dog while the end of Lola's song had played and the next started. This one had a Celtic dirge for a background. They were mesmerizing. "This way," Eva murmured.

Rows of black candles in stands, bowls, containers of all kinds lined the walls, hundreds of them. No electric lights lit the room; instead it was bright with the flickerings of all the candles. The room could be a ballroom. Some three dozen people milled around in clumps, talking and clutching cocktail and wine glasses. It felt like a party, though no one seemed to be kicking it up too much. The conversations drifted to us as low murmurs.

Ebbie stood near the hallway. He gave us one of his waves over toward a bar where the man with the ponytail who I had seen at the funeral stood talking with two very young ladies in matching black velvet gowns.

Levi looked up from his conversation and saw us. I expected a reaction, but not the one we got. It would not have surprised me for us both to be tossed out on our ears. But he opened his arms and came to us. "Eva," he called out. His gestures were expansive, dramatic.

Eva looked as cautious as me. But she accepted the hug and returned it.

"You seem willing to share my personal space with the strangest people," he said to Eva. He made it sound like a jest, but his eyes locked with hers in a struggle of wills that threw sparks.

Eva stared back at him, neither laughing nor responding.

"You must excuse me," Levi said. The corners of his mouth lifted. "I do not have the acquaintance of your friend." Those were his exact words, with enough eye-roll spin on them to let us know he believed the stilted way of speaking about as much as we did.

He moved close to me. I'm a good six feet tall. But my eyes clicked up to look into his. I noticed that all the men in the party ran to height, though I did not see a basketball hoop in the room. All the men also wore dark clothes. Except for being rumpled, my suit fit right in.

Levi stared at me. His eyes were naturally wide and unblinking. His intensity felt, well, palpable.

"Levi, this is Travis."

I stood as close as I had ever been to him. He had a long narrow face, on which the skin looked pale—and not a healthy pale. The flesh on the rest of him, the meat and muscle of him, appeared to be fading from his bones, decaying. I half expected him to smell of rotting, for his breath to be the foul stench of decay. Yet when he held a bony hand out, he surprised me with the strength of his grip. His hand felt hard and as grasping as a claw of steel when I shook it. He shook only just long enough. His eyes never left mine, nor flickered. He leaned slightly closer. "What is it that you do?"

I let my eyes click away from his, noticed that he held a wine glass in his left hand. The liquid in it was the color and consistency of blood. I did not know of any wines that looked like that. I had to wonder at his brass if he walked around with a glass of blood, though it *was* his house. He held the glass with his fingers cradling the bowl, the stem between his long fingers, the way you would hold a brandy snifter. He lifted his glass slowly, took a small sip. As he lowered it, a small drop of red clung to the corner of his mouth. A pale, pointed, pink tongue darted out to sweep the drop away. I repressed a shudder.

"I'm a finder," I said, looking back up into those unwavering eyes. "I find things."

"That is so . . . interesting. For people?"

I nodded.

"What sort of things?"

"Lost things, solutions to things, missing things."

"Are you good at it?"

"I have my days."

I started to wonder if they had any hundred-percent blue agave tequila at the bar I could see if I took a half step to my right and peered past his shoulder. That's when I saw Cassie.

Her eyes swept across me and she turned away to talk to someone else at the bar. She wore a red satin strapless gown, her blond hair hanging in a wave down the back. I had never seen her dressed in anything but her uniform or jeans. She was something to see in a gown. I forced my attention back to Levi. His intense eyes locked again with mine. It felt draining to be near the man. Maybe that is where some of the original vampire business began. To look at him, black suit and pale skin, with his self-absorbed demeanor, I could see how someone might very well begin to believe he had dark powers, or that he was the devil.

"You," a voice shouted, shrill and upset. I turned to see the face pointed toward mine. "You're a friend of that damned Owen Peasey." It was Lila.

She pushed one fellow aside as she shoved through the small crowd to us. Surrounded, as we were, by the sound of Lola's perfect voice doing songs I had never heard, Lila's voice, even in speaking, sounded harsh, and like a large rat being pulled through a small hole.

"You heard he fired me, didn't you?"

Heads turned toward the disturbance. Levi made a barely perceptible nod to two of the men. They came up to either side of Lila, stood beside her.

"You can't muzzle me. You know that . . ."

Levi stepped forward, bent close and whispered into the

woman's ear. Whatever he said made her face wash white all the way down into her plunging cleavage. She nodded, became as quiet as a stone, let the men lead her away. They moved briskly with her through the crowd and were soon out of the room.

Levi came back to join us. He watched me, if anything, more closely. "She had neither the voice, nor the disposition for music. It was a mistake for her to let herself become involved. I thought I did her a favor, but I erred."

She did start to make Lola look like an easygoing person. Owen had summed her up by saying to me, "As I slide down the banister of life, I will remember Lila as a splinter in my ass." Levi glanced to the back of the room.

He said to me, "If you can excuse me, I wish to go and see that she is not too uncomfortable." He spun and glided away. If he had been wearing a cape it would have fluttered gracefully behind him.

His being hospitable gave me the same unease I got from the detectives Barnett and Kilgallon trying to be the good guys.

Eva had drifted over to a small circle of people and chatted. My eyes swept the room, saw a flash of red as a gown slipped through side doors into what looked like a library.

I wove through the people with the ease of someone at a cocktail party who knows almost none of the other participants. I glanced around, then slipped through the doorway into the next room.

Cassie stood alone. She spun a globe with her fingers while she glanced around the room. I thought she was looking at the rows of leather-bound books that filled shelves that lined every wall. Then I realized she was checking for cameras.

I looked around. A fireplace, dark wooden shelves that ran to the ceiling, a sliding ladder that let you climb to the upper rows, a deep hunter green carpet, thick leather-covered wing chairs. Low flames of a real wood fire crackled in the fireplace.

A pair of matched dueling pistols lay crisscrossed on the mantel.

"I understand that Levi always wanted to be rich," she said, "but never wanted to work. Looks like he did rather well."

I saw a whole row of books on alchemy, but did not think that was how he had acquired his wealth. I moved over beside the fireplace. It was a big one. A person could nearly stand in it if the low fire had not been lit to compete against the fierce air-conditioning. Levi kept his home about the temperature of Vito's morgue.

"Where have you been?" Cassie gave the globe another spin. She looked up at me from lowered eyes.

"Here and there."

"Who's the woman?"

"A fortune-teller."

"I hope you haven't settled."

I wanted to clear my throat, but fought the urge. "What do you make of Levi?"

"Like I said, he's rich."

"How did he get that way?"

"Some desire, others pursue."

I said, "After a while, Ruth left the room. Then things got ruthless."

"No," Cassie agreed. "He didn't get it by kissing babies. Though I hear that's where Ortega leans. But there's money around here, a big liquid lump of it." She looked around the room like it might be laying in a pile in some corner. I did not grow any keener about how similar her eyes were to Joz's when she squinted that way.

Cassie stepped close enough to reach and straighten my tie. She closed a button on my shirt, smoothed the shirt and jacket front with her hand. I watched her eyes for any glitter. I don't know what there is about a woman seeing a man with another woman, even if it is a man she has tossed aside like a bone, but some spark of a formerly smoldering ember will flash.

She looked up into my eyes, said, "We had better get back and mingle before we're missed."

"How did you manage to crash this shindig?"

"Now think, Trav. How did *you* get in?" I had not seen her with any of the other men. She must have cozied up to Levi himself, a course that had to be more dangerous than I liked to think about for her. She spun and walked away.

Eva was looking around for me when I came back into the room. She bustled over and looped an arm through mine. "I thought I'd lost you."

"Nearly did," I said. "You done socializing?"

"Gosh, does this mean you take me home now?"

Levi came back into the room. His intensity had become a brief flicker compared to before. His mind was elsewhere. He turned on a heel and started toward one of the small crowds.

The two of us moved to where Levi had stopped. He gave us a nod, seemed ready to turn to another group of people. I said, "That's Lola, isn't it?"

His head panned back to me. I nodded at a corner of the room, since I could see no speakers.

"Yes." He glanced at Eva.

"How did you get these unreleased songs?"

"We were friends. Very good friends."

"Members of the same club?" I said. I might have well have said cult. His eyes widened and he stepped close to me, leaned in, invading my space from a couple of angles. It is not always what a man like Levi does in front of you that impresses you that he is raw evil, even if it is wringing the necks of young kittens. Words like aggression, competition, lacked the punch to describe the way he looked into me.

Looking into his hypnotic wide black eyes I knew clearly and completely for the first time that he had no limits, none at all.

He possessed the savage youth to tear at the world with his teeth if that's what it took, and he was unflinchingly ready to do it if that's what he needed to do to get rich, or to eliminate anyone who threatened him. At some note in the overhead music his eyes flicked away from me.

"Good night, Eva," he said, without looking at me.

"We'd better go," Eva said. Her arm tightened on mine.

Outside, the moon had become, if anything, more full. It looked large enough to see lines of detail, craters—whatever face the moon possessed. It did not look happy, might have even had a sinister scowl. I could have been influenced by the setting I left behind me.

We stepped out around the row of parked cars to get to where I had parked. I saw two heads in a darkened car across from us, put a hand out to stop Eva, felt it press across her soft chest.

"Can it wait until we get home?"

"Shhh."

"What?"

"It's okay, Travis," a scratchy voice came from the car. "It's us."

I moved closer; Eva clung tighter to my arm.

"Borster," I said. "Findlay. What are you fellows doing staked out on your night off? This the way you double-date?"

Borster's pockmarked and scarred face looked up at me, the moonlight catching every unemotional line of his face. Findlay's chuckle broke into a cough that sounded like a hurt seal.

"You should get in touch with your new homicide chums," Borster said. His voice came out flat enough to stand on.

"If you mean Barnett and Kilgallon, they're no chums of mine."

"They would probably enjoy speaking with you tonight. There's been a fracas."

I waited, felt a shiver run through Eva where she pressed

against my side. I pulled myself from her and leaned closer to the car. "What do you mean?"

"You should take a look for yourself. Little place down in Southeast Austin, called Eddie Paul's Wrecks. Do you need the address?"

"No," I said. "I don't."

The phone was ringing. Hard to tell how long.

In a yellow-capsule Nembutal fog, in the dark room, Leroy Hunt reached to the bedside table, fumbled for the receiver.

"Hello. Hello."

He heard singing. A woman's voice:

"What I thought I needed, I let go.
Oh, I miss it all somehow.
Can't recover, can't beg out,
The devil has it now."

"Lola. Is that you? Lola?" He realized what he had said. He threw down the phone, and scrambled to claw his way out of the bed.

CHAPTER THIRTEEN

I let Eva off at her place on the way, with barely enough time for her to step out and swing the passenger door shut. "Well," she huffed. I pressed on the gas heading down into what the police department calls the "F" or Frank Sector. I could see flashing lights from half-a-dozen blocks away as I turned onto the street where about a lifetime ago, it felt, I had dropped off Jose Doe's mother and trailed her to the auto wrecking yard.

Some of the lights came from EMS vehicles. Even a fire truck or two had been called to the scene. I meant to park as far away as I could, but before I could ease over I got waved around the row of flashing vehicles by a cop in uniform. To him I was "through traffic" trying to get past. He meant to get me the hell through with a minimum of rubbernecking.

Halfway down the row of vehicles, someone shouted my name. I saw Barnett and Kilgallon push past a couple of firemen. They came out between a fire truck and an ambulance to wave me to a stop. When I had stopped, they came around to the driver's side.

"What do you have," Barnett said, "a police antenna up your butt?"

"You're closer than you think."

"You didn't get that bullet hole on your passenger side tonight, did you?" Kilgallon said. "Looks like a warning shot to me."

"You think this guy's bright enough to take a warning?" Barnett asked Kilgallon. He turned back to me. "What *are* you doing here?"

That led to me having to pull over and go through about forty questions, all of which I was unable or unwilling to answer.

They might have kept grilling me until dawn. But Barnett's head lifted and he stopped in mid-sentence. He looked past me toward the wrecking yard. Kilgallon had gone the way of the deepwater clam as well. Both stood silent and waiting. I had to turn and look.

As soon as the two men coming toward us saw me look their way, they had out their IDs in the prescribed FBI-wannabe manner. But these guys were INS.

"Jacobus. Len Jacobus." Just the way you'd say James Bond. "This is Miles." I guessed that Miles didn't have another half to his name, or that it mattered too little to share. "Could we have a few words with you?"

"What was the other choice?" I asked. Barnett and Kilgallon both gave short deliberate nods, then moved away into the hubbub that surrounded us.

"We've been by your place a couple of times. You're not in much, huh?" Jacobus did all the talking for this pair. Jacobus looked lean and barely into his thirties. His hair had been buzzed into a short flat-top, his suit a dark off-green. His eyes had a natural narrowness to them, set high in his long face. His cheeks had sucked in hollows, with lines like commas on either side of his mouth. I didn't think he got the lines from laughing. He had all the tact of a freshly promoted Second Lieutenant, the kind that got bullets in the back of their skulls in Viet Nam.

His partner, Miles, besides making the Sphinx seem on the windy side, looked older. His hair was short and gray, his build low and rounded. He wore a brown suit and looked like someone close to a pension, but not close enough. He had a Hispanic cast to his features and an air of Judas about him, of which he seemed overly aware. He looked like someone sliding sideways through his personal midlife crisis and he wasn't going to make it worse by trying to speak when his partner had the floor.

"What was it you wanted to see me about?" I asked.

Jacobus glanced behind himself to where a pair of EMS workers carried another covered body out of the wrecking yard. A smell of something burning wafted toward us, not a big fire, but no one's campfire either.

"We're investigating trafficking in illegal aliens. Your name has come up a time or two."

"As a trafficker?"

"No. We didn't mean to imply that. But you have left tracks. Do you mind telling us what you know about any of this?" He waved an expansive hand back at the area enclosed in yellow tape.

"No more than you do."

"I must remind you that I'm here in an official capacity. And on a personal note, I am almost never amused."

Miles looked away, as if an expression might flit across his face.

Jacobus struck me as dangerous, in the way that government bean-counters can get if they get a half inch of authority. He gave me a look he must have thought appeared insightful, even sly. "You did some work for Armando Manuel de Ortega. We have tracked Armando's efforts for some time. This little site here had become one of the centers for those he brought in. Ortega is something of an importer. You knew that, didn't you?"

"What do you want to know, specifically?"

"Why, everything. We want you to share all you have gathered. Let us decide what is important. Don't hold back a thing."

It rocked me back on my heels. I looked closer to see if he thought he'd made a joke. Not a chance. This gazooney actually expected a private detective to get sudden diarrhea of the mouth just because he had flashed a piece of cardboard.

"You fellows are paid by the government, the same one I pay taxes to, aren't you?" I steamed forward before he could let out so much as a bubble. "And you're a professional, aren't you, Jacobus?"

"Where do you think you're going with . . . ?"

"Then do your own homework." I spun and headed back toward the street. Neither of them called out to stop me.

Somewhere around two in the morning I got back into my car and headed for Vito's office.

A crew was just bringing in two more bodies as I arrived. I waited in the parking lot until the EMS crew got back into their van, turned off their flashing lights, and pulled away.

I slipped inside the building, went down the familiar hallway, nearly got turned away when I'd pushed through the swinging doors until Vito spotted me and called off the assistant.

"Oh, let him in. He's no reporter. He gives us too much trouble we'll do an autopsy on him too."

A row of bodies had been lined up on gurneys waiting for whatever happens next. They were not all men. I saw at least one woman and child. I counted six bodies before Vito waved me into his office.

"I hope you don't want to sleep here tonight, because we're going to be up to our elbows until dawn."

"Don't let me keep you from your work."

"That's okay. I don't like to work on them while they're still warm. This volume means we can write off bringing in more help, too. They can do the prepping. What do you know about all this?"

"Almost nothing. I spoke with Barnett and Kilgallon, got less than nothing from them. I was hoping *you* could help."

"Do you have anything to smoke?" He rummaged around in

the drawers of his desk, throwing each open and digging around before slamming it closed.

"Sorry."

He slammed the center drawer shut, ignored a couple of crumpled sheets that stuck out.

"I doubt there will ever be an official version on this one," he said. "The public will have to do with whatever creative twist the media is up to. And believe me, they're spinning hard and fast already. The first question was about holes in any necks. There aren't."

"What do *you* make of it?"

"Looks like two camps going at it."

"Levi on the one side, Ortega on the other?"

"Sounds about right."

"Of course, Ortega's just the front man, maybe Levi as well."

"Of course."

"Levi's side being the one using voodoo or this vampire scare crap to keep his own people in line and encroach on those who were imported by Ortega."

Vito nodded. He jumped up, rushed out of the room, came back a moment later with a cigarette over his ear and holding another. He broke off the filter of the cigarette he held, turned it around and lit the shaggy end. "Forgot Paul smokes. One of the assistants."

"You think we're done with the vampire business? None of these had any blood missing did they?"

"There was blood enough, but none of it missing, no. No neck holes either. Probably wasn't time for any of that."

"All the earlier victims of anything that looked like vampire work came from the wrecking yard, didn't they? The floater. Jose Doe."

"Looks that way."

"Except for the fighting, and a number of deaths, have you

found anything that ties to the stuff I was onto earlier?"

"Well, there was a dead goat."

"Goat?"

"I thought it could've happened earlier in the battle. I'm not gonna do an autopsy on a goat."

"You don't think those in the yard might've been in the early stages of a barbecue when they were interrupted?"

"I don't think anyone was thinking about bar-bee-damn-que when *this* broke out. Not the way the goat must've dragged its insides along for yards through the lot before dying. That's not how you dress out a goat. A pure black one, I might add."

"Which side was warning which?"

"Doesn't even matter. It's enough to tell me we've got a connection here."

"Knowing what you do," I said, "who do you think killed Lola, maybe Watt Stoner as well?"

"Now that," Vito said, puffing up at the blank ceiling, "is the conundrum that is still yours to solve."

I pried my eyes apart to the sound of someone yelling in high-pitched Spanish about wanting to get the rooms cleaned and get out of there. The room I occupied could use another coat of paint, and perhaps thicker walls. You could buy the furnishings out the back door of a furniture warehouse without, perhaps, breaking a hundred-dollar bill. It was no Waldorf-Astoria, but it beat trying to sleep in the all-night theaters. Too many restless men there want to be friends.

By the time I had showered and slipped out of the room, all of the other rooms must have been cleaned with only mine remaining. The cleaning lady leaned against her cart and gave me the evil eye as I staggered out into the bright sunlight.

"Lo siento," I said, sorry to mess up her life by my trying to carve out four hours of sleep in a room I shared with varied

representatives of the insect world.

The newspaper headlines grabbed my eye. I went over to the box by the motel's office and shoved in a couple of quarters, drew out a copy. NIGHT OF TERROR seemed to overstate it. Ten people had died, at least twenty had been taken to hospitals. I was relieved to see that, for once, no mention was made of vampires. The paper talked of war, but did not say between whom. An editorial inside as much as advised the police to drop whatever else they were working on, except that zippy vampire thing, and tend to this. The cops had been a good-sized pain to me so far, but from now on I sensed they would be worse.

I climbed into my car and started off for breakfast in whatever greasy spoon caught my fancy. The sky, though it had gotten to midday, had a soapy, uncertain look. Austin is a city that is most often dominated by bright sunlight and blue skies. My own mood may have been to blame for the way I saw things. I heard low soft murmurs of music in my head, which is not unusual when in the Live Music Capital of America.

Traffic was no longer the Gordian knot it can be in the early A.M. Still, I seemed to get stuck behind every Volvo in town, almost forgot for the moment that I drove one myself. I had the usual restless itch of a case unsolved. I felt no closer to finding who had done in Lola, and now the footprints were cluttered with some sort of local Hispanic civil war. I usually do very well, thank you, being on my own. Maybe I had gotten lonely. I had never thought too much about it before, but then I hadn't had Cassie, Joz, Borster and Findlay, Ortega, Barnett and Kilgallon, and now the INS circling around my casa like vultures on a holiday.

Outside the diner I selected for my moment of haute cuisine—a little place on the corner of Second and Congress where I could get huevos rancheros at any hour of the day—I dropped coins into the phone and dialed Jimmy Bravuro's number. He wasn't in, but his answering service gave me his rough coordinates for later that afternoon. I hung up and looked around at a day that did not look like it was improving. Then I went inside the restaurant to add hot sauce to the mix.

"They hit us hard, Mr . . ."

"No names on the phone. You know . . ."

"What you theenk?"

"Listen to you. Don't speak like that. Next thing you'll be saying 'stinking moniees.' "

"But what? You wan' us to close down a while?"

"You run a simple services business, Armando. That's all. Why would you stop doing that?"

"But, you wan' us to hit back?"

"I'll let you know."

CHAPTER FOURTEEN

You run a little PI agency like mine out of the shirt on your back, without the benefit of checking in at an office now and again, and you end up doing a lot of the chores, unless you have a friend or two who can take on a task for hire. I headed to the south end of town to see what I could learn about how Levi made the kind of money he had. A credit union connection named Lori sat in her sweatshop sweating when I came into her small strip-mall office on Barton Springs Road.

She looked up from between twin towers of folders on either corner of the desk. Another lay open in front of her. Lori had long brown hair, tied and hanging down her back. Her face always looked cheerful and almost free of makeup. She looked up at me, headset on, talking into a phone. Her right hand took notes while her left hand reached for a large jar of Tums. When she saw me she gave me an eye roll. I didn't know whether it meant I owed her sympathy for the person she spoke with, or if it was about me bugging her, maybe both. I moved a newspaper and small pile of books off a chair and sat to wait.

Lori had two kids and another on the way. I had helped her out with an ex-boyfriend turned stalker. You would think that once a woman has had children with another man that a fellow could adjust to the idea that her commitment had moved elsewhere. Bill Roy Williams had either not been a quick study or had been influenced by the case or so of beer he drank daily. He had been a hard person to convince. Yet I was able to learn he had made off with his church's youth activity fund and lost the whole thing in the commodities market. I had helped gather evidence enough for his arrest. He ended up with time on his hands and a chance to shake his beer habit. When he got out—and his parole was coming up—we would see how he would do back in the world. I hoped he had gotten over the idea of bothering Lori.

She hung up and flipped a switch. Then she tugged off the headset. "That'll handle the calls for a spell. You still on that case you called me about?"

"When I asked you about Hunt?"

"Yeah."

"Same case."

"I told you, he handles a lot of deals for Jake Hunger, lives quite well on the scraps."

"How's Jake Hunger make his money?"

"He *has* money. They say that if you have a hundred dollars that it's no guarantee that you can turn it into a hundred and ten dollars. But if you have a hundred million dollars, it's not very hard at all for that to become a hundred and ten million."

"I guess I'll just have to trust you on that."

"So, what drags your carcass down to Bubba country this time?"

"I need a favor."

She pursed her lips, but hesitated only a second. "Fire away."

"I want to know how a fellow named Levi Damocles made the kind of money he has."

Her pencil had leaped to life against a pad while I spoke. "And?"

"What he's worth now, that sort of thing. I know you have your ways. And, oh, that other fellow. Jake Hunger. I'd like to know even more about him."

"Trav, I don't think you want to mess around with someone

like Jake Hunger."

"Bad medicine?"

"The worst. For you. He chews up little guys and spits them out. You wouldn't even be an hors d'oeuvre to him."

"If you can, see what you can dig up without risking yourself."

"Travis, I fear what one of these days I'm gonna read on page one about you. But I'll do it. You might could do me a turn. I'm stuck in here. Betty Lou's took the day off. Could you be a sweetheart and step to the diner half a block down and get me two BLTs, a malt, two fries, and snag one of those whole gherkins they have?"

When my head rocked back, she said, "I'm eating for two, Travis. Now hop to it. I'm starvin'."

Forty minutes later, after waiting at the counter and carrying back enough food for four or five people, I entered the office again and put the bulging sacks on her desk. She wrapped up the call she was on, rigged the headset for automatic answering again. Then she cleared away a few files and began to eat.

As a rule I am a hearty fellow, have watched crowds in riot and seen the aftermath of many a crime. I had to look away while Lori ate.

For the first five minutes or so she did some serious eating. I picked up a magazine, did not notice until flipping through a few pages that it was from a year back. Most of it seemed news to me, though.

"I don't know if this Levi fellow has the kind of money you think he does," Lori said when the windmill of her jaws slowed a bit.

"He seems to be living large enough."

"From what I could find," she wiped a bit of mayo from the corner of her lips, "he brings in no more than a hundred to two hundred K a year."

"Which isn't peanuts. But he lives like he has more than that.

His house is three stories and must have a dozen bedrooms. Inside it's all Italian marble, real paintings, and leather furniture."

"His sole source of income seems to be from a handful of landscaping firms, lawn care really and maid services. He owns a couple of greenhouses and his home. But I see what you mean. It sounds like a pretty expensive home."

"He could be only claiming part of his income."

"Do you think?" She looked up, let her face twist into a duh look. "If he thinks he can get away with that he should talk to Willie Nelson's accountants."

"If he is, I'm surprised the IRS isn't hovering around his place."

"How do you know they aren't?"

I said, "The INS may be looking his way too. I know they have an eye on his competition."

"The paper trail I saw on his financial side tells me that he keeps a pretty low profile."

I thought of the black suits, the glass of perhaps blood. Someone living a low profile is not how I would have described Levi after meeting him. "What about Jake Hunger?"

"I told you . . ."

"I know. But I've got to go there. What do you know?"

"He's a local power nut. He's tried politics before, was very big against NAFTA."

I must have looked puzzled. Lori said, "That's the North American Free Trade Agreement. Jake Hunger leaned the same way Ross Perot did when it was introduced. They thought it gave away American jobs to people below the border."

"What else do you have on him?"

"Sorry you weren't paying attention to the news for the past few years. He ran for the office of U.S. representative, then state representative—didn't make either of those. He went for city councilman, got that. Some say it cost him more than it was worth."

"Guess it's the old question of why anyone rich would want a position of public service. What else?"

"Wife's dead. He has two daughters, both married. Ima Dodson and Lilian Obregón. He's worth somewhere around thirty or forty million. Not real rich by Texas standards, but well off. You know the story, don't you, about the cattle rancher who said he'd lost a few thousand head but didn't get hurt like the big boys?"

I said, "I know about one methadone clinic. In what else does Jake Hunger have his money?"

"Oh, this and that. Mostly real estate, developments, office buildings, smaller businesses like the clinic you mention. I imagine he has a handful of people he trusts who help him keep the money moving. He's usually busy pounding the table at one meeting or another. He's the kind who likes that sort of involvement, which is why you should stay the hell away from him."

"Thanks. I know you mean well."

"You won't think I'm joking if you go crossways of him."

The temperature had progressed to eighty degrees by the time I left Lori's office. My jacket didn't cling to me by the time I climbed into the car, but I felt warm. I pulled the door closed with one hand while I started it and hoped the AC felt frisky. I pulled out into traffic as if I had someplace to go. So far I was learning a lot, but not moving forward.

Sometimes when a case seems to be going in more circles than a dog chasing its own tail the best plan for me is to take a deep breath and go back to the beginning. I made a U-turn at the next light and headed toward the Catholic church where Lola and Levi had once been parochial students. There were a few things I had not asked her about this cult business.

It took me ten minutes, but I found a spot where I could park in the shade. I got out of the car, went to the church, found that Sister Consuela was visiting people over at St. David's Hospital, went back to the car, got in and headed there.

Visiting hours were in progress when I entered the building, something of a new thing for me. I didn't catch hell from Ginny, the head nurse, this time.

"Have you seen . . . ?" It was as far as I got.

Ginny rushed around from behind her station, came over to me and gave me a hug. Nothing she could have done could have stunned me more.

"Fancy you comin' here. Figures, though. Have you heard?"

"Heard what?"

"He came to. That young boy you were looking in on. It's the most wonderful . . . I suppose I should call the police. They asked me to when . . . Oh, it can wait. Come on." She grabbed my upper arm and tugged me down the hall.

Inside the room, Sister Consuela looked up at me from beside the bed where she was bent close to Jose Doe. His eyes were open, blinking around at the room and at us. "He's back with us," Sister Consuela said.

I went down on one knee beside the bed so that my face could be close to his. I hoped I could get some scrap before the police questioned him.

He looked at me, as did Sister Consuela from her side of his bed. "You some kinda Chota?" he asked, his voice still scratchy from not using it for a while. There was more color in his face than I had seen the last time I was here.

"No," I said. I looked up, saw Ginny giving me the eye, wondering if I had been too much for him to wake up to.

I said, "What do you remember, before you woke up here? I mean about what happened."

"There was some guys . . ."

"Gang?"

"No. I know all the colors and signs. These was just some guys I wasn't clicked up with."

"Was there a fight?"

"A little scuffle."

"You get knocked out?"

"I don' know. Must've."

"Nothing after that?"

"No, just wakin' up here."

"Any reason for the scuffle? You with a gang?"

"I'm no banger. I talked wit' the Cholos once. But I boned outta that. I'm a solo dude."

"Why the scuffle then?"

"I don' know. Maybe it's 'cause where I'm from."

"In Mexico?"

"No. Where I live now."

Ginny butted in. "Travis, that's all I can . . ."

I stood up. I held out a hand. "Get well," I said. I had gotten more than I expected. He lifted his hand slowly, gave mine a soft slap, no force in it.

From where I stood I could see out into the hallway. There she stood, her bucket on the floor, her hands up to the sides of her face. I was glad to see she had not been hurt in all the shooting the other night. Tears poured down both cheeks. How she had managed to keep from running into the room was beyond me. I wiggled a finger at Ginny, leaned closer when she came near. I whispered into her ear.

"His mother?" she said before I could stop her. Her head had snapped back.

I hushed her and leaned close again, whispered and pointed out the door. Ginny's head panned to the doorway. She took in the cleaning woman standing there. Then Ginny looked back at me. "Travis, you never cease to amaze me. How did you . . . ?"

I gave a head nudge toward the hallway.

"Okay," Ginny said. She went out into the hall, came back with the cleaning woman. Jose tried to sit up in bed when he saw her, but he was too weak for that. She rushed over to the bed. Their arms went out and they hugged each other. Both were speaking rapidly in Spanish, too fast for me to follow. I did catch that his name was Esteban, which moved him from his Jose Doe status.

Ginny looked at me, then turned her head and rubbed a finger at the corner of one eye. Sister Consuela looked at me like I had just walked across water, at least a small puddle.

The three of us moved out into the hallway to let Esteban catch up with his mother, who had managed to be near him for the duration of his coma.

"We lose so many who never do come out," Ginny said, her professional face back in place. "It's nice when one pulls through. You can't believe all the blood and intravenous fluids we've pumped through him. I don't know what finally snapped him out of it."

Sister Consuela's eyes shown with an inner radiance. She said nothing.

"You're looking full of sparkle today, Sister Consuela," I said.

"Now, Travis," Ginny said. "I hope you aren't making a pass at a person of the cloth."

"Thought of dating a nun once," I admitted, "but I didn't think I could get into the habit."

The sharp pain in my ribs came from Ginny's elbow. She went back in the room, told the mother that Esteban needed some rest, that she could come back later.

Esteban's mother recognized me when Ginny led her from the room. All she knew about me was that I had given her a lift home once, and that I had gone to bat with Ginny so that she could be with her son now that he was out of his coma.

"Buen hombre," she said. A person could have that on a headstone and feel pretty okay about it. Her face still shone wet with tears. She held the green scarf she had had tied over her hair in one hand. Her arms opened and she came and wrapped them around me in a hug. I was sure getting the hugs today.

I leaned down close. *"Los Olvidados?"* I said. That's the name the crowd living in the junkyard went by, "the forgotten ones," from some old Mexican movie, I figured.

She pulled back to arm's length, pointed to herself.

"No. *Los otros.*"

When she said it I could see her relive some of the moments of horror that evening. She had the same ideas I had about who had attacked the wrecking yard.

She leaned closer and whispered. It took a couple of tries on her part. My Spanish has never been my strong suit. But at last I had a handle on the rough location. *"Gracias,"* I said.

Esteban's mother went back to her bucket and mop, pulled on her scarf, and with one last look into the hospital room she turned and started up the long hallway. I may have been imagining it, but there seemed to be more lift to her steps.

"There are days," Ginny sighed, "that make up for the others."

"I must go," Sister Consuela said. "There are other visits I must make."

"Come on," I said. "Give me one for the road."

Sister Consuela tilted her head in thought, then said, "The journey is the reward."

A soft muted cornet played, rifting up only to fall in a flutter of notes to a moaning growl.

The music was always lonely, but he could not say sad. It had been with him as long as he could recall.

CHAPTER FIFTEEN

I found the Limping Duck Recording Studio in an ochre-colored stucco building down on South Lamar Street, nestled in the halfhearted shade of an eighteen-foot-tall Palo Verde tree sprouting out of the gravel parking lot. A redbrick dry cleaning building nestled close on the other side. I stepped out of my air-conditioned car and waded through the spongy air that had been left behind by the recent rainy season.

Double glass doors I had to struggle to push open led into a waiting area. I saw no receptionist. In a low budget set-up like this, that would be a luxury.

A red light was on over one door at the rear of the foyer. I opened the other door, expecting a broom closet for all I knew.

Sound boomed out at me. Two different people held up a hand to warn me to keep quiet. One warning came from a technician in front of a wide board covered with what looked like sliding pegs. The other fellow wore a large headset, watched gauges on a wall of lights, meters, and turning reels of tape.

Jimmy Bravuro sprawled across a chair in the corner, leaning back against the wall, his feet up on a folding chair in front of him. He gave me a thumbs up, lifted a chair and lowered it beside his, making sure the whole operation made no sound.

I sat down in the offered chair, looked through the glass wall where Jonesy stood in the soundproofed room. His head was tilted back as he sang up into the black fist of a microphone.

He strummed his guitar and sang:

As lost in a crowd as a tear in the rain,
Left craving feeling, if only just pain.

We waited until the song vibrated to a close. The guy with the headset held up a hand, then lowered it. The technician at the board slid his double handful of pegs slowly up in a fade.

"What do you think?" he said to Jimmy.

"Darrell's singing and guitar work were never part of the problem. But he seems to believe in what he's singing this time. The words are better than anything on either of those last two CDs."

"They were that bad?" I said.

The guy taking off his headset said, "To call them doggerel would be an insult to dogs."

Jonesy pushed into the room. He held his guitar in one hand. "Well, well, well," he said when he spotted me, "if it isn't the detective to Austin's music industry stars."

I held up a hand, guilty as charged.

" 'Lo, Jimmy," Jonesy said, still wired enough for someone to string up Christmas lights across his wiry frame. He spun to the recording crew. "How was it, Rob? Stu?"

"Sounded like the real stuff," Rob said. He had worn the headset.

"We'll know more after next Monday's session," Stu said. "But we might well be on record pace toward one killer bee of a CD."

Jonesy turned back to us, a slow smile spreading across his face. He looked at me, said, "What're you doing here, by the way? Is Jimmy helping you with your case?"

I was going to offer a footnote on the war going on out there. But Jimmy beat me.

"Well, yes and no," Jimmy said. "I'm supposed to be helping, but I haven't been much good to Trav."

"Maybe there's something I can do?" Jonesy looked ready to

leap outside and settle the fray himself.

"I don't think so, Darrell." I reached up to try to push my unruly hair into place. "But if you can, anything is welcome at this stage. I came here hoping to pick Jimmy's brain about the political scene."

"You're not just barking up the wrong tree there, Trav," Jimmy said. "You're in the wrong forest."

"Is there a political angle to the case?" Jonesy asked.

"I don't know. But there's a power one. Usually the politics isn't far behind, if not the money people behind the politicians."

Jonesy gave a sigh, looked down at the guitar he held. "I feel sorry for people to whom money is their god."

Jimmy looked over at me. "Spike Milligan used to say that you can't buy friends with money, but it can get you a higher class of enemy."

"I think all that matters," Jonesy said, leaning toward a philosophical track I was afraid he felt needed sharing, "is having a shot at a dream. Oh, I used to wonder where I got off thinking I had anything to share that the world needed. After all, my music isn't going to save lives or even make the world a better place—no Nobel prizes waiting for me. Maybe all I need is an occasional thanks and a handful of fans."

Jimmy gave me an awkward grin.

"We had better get going," I said, louder than I had intended.

Jimmy rose. Jonesy left the room to put away his guitar. I asked Rob, "How did you guys come to drop by the Devil's Due and hear Jonesy in the first place?"

Rob glanced at Stu, who shrugged. Rob said, "We were in a financial tough spot, got a little slack from the guy who held the vise grips if we would go over and listen to Lola Pillacherosi. Turns out we ended up listening to Darrell instead."

"Was this guy you speak of named Hunt?"

Rob glanced at Stu, then back at me. He nodded slowly.

Out in the parking lot the air had dried. The sun beat down on my forehead. Jimmy stood looking at me with his thumbs hooked into the top of his jeans. "Now what *are* you here about?" he said. Figure him for knowing he's no political expert, that I'd been blowing smoke inside. The case centered around Lola was still a music industry one the way I saw it. I just had a lot going on to the side.

"I need to ask a favor."

"Ask."

"Do you think it would be all right if I flop at your place tonight?"

"I don't know, Trav."

"What do you mean? Is it yes, or no?"

"Well . . . okay. Sure. My pad is your casa. Who are you dodging? If it's the IRS, my place may not suit you as much as you think."

"You seem to give those boys a lot of thought lately."

"Look how they treated poor Willie."

"I spotted a couple of cars staked out around my office. I haven't been back there in a while."

"Who?"

"My good friend, Borster, the cop, who you've met in the usual unpleasant circumstances. Another car was filled with the finer element from below the border. I might have ticked off someone in that camp."

"Well . . ."

"Oh, and Joz Brosche and Cassie Winnick might be camped out inside the office for all I know."

"Oh, I don't think so, Trav."

"They might be. They were when I last looked."

"You give them a key, or what?"

I frowned at him. He would know that Joz did not need keys.

He said, "I thought you and Cassie were on some kind of squeeze level?"

"That's over. You know that."

"So now you're dodging her, huh?"

"Seems that way. Now, how about it? Is it a problem?"

"I said okay." He seemed hesitant. "You're a bit antsy. You get into something bigger than you thought? You don't have anything to do with this Hispanic civil war that spread all over page one of today's newspaper, do you?"

"I'm in the wings on that one."

"But liable to be dragged to center stage?"

"Possible. Why don't we talk about it when we get to your place instead of out here in the heat?" I could feel a trickle of sweat running down my spine.

"I hope you know what you're doing, Trav. What old Amarillo Slim used to say was, you sit down to the poker table and you don't spot the sucker, you should get up and leave. 'Cause likely as not the sucker is you."

"Can we just go to your place?" The words came out as a tired sigh.

"Oh, sure. Just follow me into the heart of South Austin— Bubba land. Sounds like you've got to be more careful about who you're mixing with." He looked at the bullet hole in the side of my car that I had not gotten around to patching yet. "I forget who said it, but the saying goes something like, never let your mouth make a contract your feet can't keep."

"You're sure one cornucopia of borrowed wit today," I said.

He winked. "Some days I'm as original as sin. Other days I just lean against the wind."

We got into our cars and pulled out into traffic; Jimmy led the way.

Jimmy zipped briskly along, weaving through the afternoon traffic headed south on Lamar. It was all I could do to hang onto a glimpse of the back of his car, and that was not made easier by some individuals taking a more contemplative approach to driving. One car wove in front of me from the left lane and slowed, to make a turn I figured, though the car showed no turn signal. A truck had me hemmed in on the left. Boxed in like that, I could imagine Jimmy getting way out of sight. I grew just short of the intellectual level where one pounds the steering wheel and screams expletives that question everything short of the heritage of fellow drivers—when I noticed the men in the truck watching me. I looked ahead, saw eyes in the rear view mirror looking at me.

The vehicle behind me was another pickup, this one crammed with more hostile faces. I saw a gap ahead between parked cars, jerked my steering wheel to the right and hopped the curb, skimmed between parking meters and gave a street bum the scare of his day as he dove to his side between parked cars. I clipped the crammed shopping cart he had left behind while making good time down the sidewalk, hoping no one stepped out of any of the businesses.

I had little time for glancing around and taking notes, but a quick look to traffic told me my move had been noticed. I came to a corner where I expected them to make their move. My plan was to swing around the corner on the sidewalk, gun the motor and squirt out at the half block, do a U-turn and head back toward traffic where I felt there would be less chance of them trying anything too blatant.

I screeched around the corner, just missing a hydrant and then a parking meter. When I straightened up I headed squarely toward a group of four men maneuvering an upright piano down a ramp into the back door of a business. They were spread across the sidewalk. Cars were parked in a row all the way to where the men stood, now frozen and looking my way. My foot hit the brake pedal with all I had. The four disc brakes did what they were supposed to do. I slide to an abrupt halt within inches of the nearest of the piano men, who it appeared had jumped the gun on his next restroom visit.

Guns bristled around me as soon as the sound and dust of my braking had died down.

One of the men yanked open the door, cut the seat belt with a knife to save me the bother of undoing it. They whisked me between the parked cars and shoved me into the back cab of an extended pickup, squished between two guys who had spent their morning having another helping of refried beans instead of bathing. Someone had thoughtfully draped an orange shop rag over the license plate, I noticed, which would make pursuit harder even if someone did get to a phone and dial 911.

"Where are we . . . ?"

An elbow smashed into my stomach in answer and to end further discussion. No one spoke during the ride. The fellow to my right took out a previously used blue bandanna. I hoped he meant to tie it around my eyes, even filthy as it was. That would mean they expected me to live. But he blew his nose and put it away. That told me they did not expect it to matter whether I knew where they were going or not.

I recognized Matt's El Ranchero and a couple of other landmarks as we wove through the city. My mood was the one you sink into when you think you might be recording a panorama for the last time.

Our little convoy pulled into a tight alley where fourteen-foot-high wooden fences lined either side and the truck could barely squeeze through. We took a sharp right turn and started down a slope. Ahead of us a pair of steel garage doors opened slowly like jaws. The driver timed our roll so that the truck just made it through. The other truck and car followed us in. The doors began to close, leaving the warehouse we had entered in heavy shadow. From the outside a wooden layer gave the building an older, run-down look. Inside, I could see the beams and framework of metal lining the walls. This was a much newer and sturdier building than it appeared from the outside.

The group unloaded from the vehicles, yanking me out and pushing me along in a stumble as we headed across the warehouse floor. Piles of cartons and boxes lined one end of the building, stolen goods for all I knew. At the other end guys stripped down cars. One crew repainted while another altered serial numbers. We started up a switch-back flight of metal stairs at the back of the warehouse that led up to a glassed-in area. Inside, the air-conditioning was turned up very high. The cold slapped me as we entered. My shirt and suit jacket clung to my back.

At the far right end of the room, sitting behind a desk that allowed him to look over the warehouse, sat Armando Manuel de Ortega. The hand holding the phone was wrapped in white tape. He hissed in low Spanish into the phone. He glanced over at us, said a couple more sharp words and slammed the receiver back onto the hook. He spun in his chair to look at me.

He reached to a walnut humidor, took out a long dark cigar. He bit the end off with his surprisingly white teeth, spit it onto the floor. For the next two or three moments we stood in silence while he took his time lighting the cigar. He gave it his full attention before looking back up to me.

"I am so glad," he said, his voice the hissing rasp one makes when sliding into quicksand, "that you could take time out from your busy day to visit me. Things will be different this time, no?"

"*I think we've seen about all the flare-up we're going to see from Los Olvidados around here.*"

"*Sir?*"

"*This situation hasn't made us look good.*"

"*What would? Shipping all of them back to Mexico?*"

"*We get any more violence and they're just not going to be so forgotten anymore.*"

"*I hope you're not forgetting that at heart most of these are humble, good, hard-working people, who are trying to survive and are being manipulated instead.*"

"*Miles, you've never spoken to me like that.*"

"*No, I . . .*"

"*Don't do it again.*"

CHAPTER SIXTEEN

Ortega's stare put a chill in me. He did not need a fire in which to slip a glowing tong to make me think the next stretch of time was not going to be all that pleasant. With him, *everything* was personal. His eyes glittered with a hate that never let up. He wore green khaki shirt and slacks, which had made him look more than a little like Castro when he had bit off the end of his thin cigar. The resemblance did not seem to be an accident.

"Was your trip here at all a discomfort?" Most of his accent was gone.

"No."

"Too bad." He took a long pull on the cigar, let the smoke trickle out slowly from his nostrils. "Perhaps we can make up for the oversight."

"What do you want with me that's worth a kidnapping rap? Shouldn't you be directing your efforts elsewhere?"

"The newspapers, the television, they all say we are at war. My people are attacked, and you want me to think of your laws?"

"You mean that mess at Eddie Paul's Wrecks? Who attacked you? What's that have to do with me?"

"We could have been friends, even allies. But you are seen in all the wrong places. And you would not help me when I asked."

"What is it you want? I trust you didn't haul me out here just to rant."

One of the men, who stood behind the chair I'd just been

slammed into, reached out. His fingers squeezed on the trapezium muscle that ran down from my neck to my shoulder. Though I anticipated the squeeze, I gave a small jump when he pinched. Wrong reaction. That seemed to please him. He squeezed harder.

"You turned down a chance to work for me. You avoid me by not going to your office. Then you show up with the other side."

"Levi? He's the other side?"

"His people attacked ours."

"How do you make that I'm linked to him? Because I was to his house?" I knew Ortega's men had been shadowing me. They would not have been able to cut off my car and bring me here if they had not been.

"I said we are at war."

"You can't always believe the media. They seem to think there are really vampires flitting around out there."

"And at war you will find I am good, very good." He ignored my input and knocked off the end of his ash onto the floor, let his eyes roll back up to me slowly.

"I think you're being gulled into something. I thought you were brighter than that."

The fellow behind me dug the fingers of both hands into my lower neck muscles. I had to fight not to jerk out of the chair.

"You think I am being stupid?"

"Give yourself all the credit you want on that." I wasn't helping myself. But they had not brought me here with any sense of ever letting me go. That was unfortunate, since for the first time I began to get some glimmer of whatever the hell was going on in town.

He stood slowly. Hands grabbed my arms and pulled them behind me. Ortega moved closer, reached out and lifted the lit end of his cigar to my face. I tried not to flinch as it neared my left eye. He lowered the tip and moved it forward, twisted it out on the skin of my left cheek.

It felt like a heated poker burning a hole clear through my cheek. I caught the smell you get at a cattle branding. I flinched inside, and had to draw on all of my purported Indian stoicism to keep from giving him the satisfaction of hearing me squeal like a fax machine.

"What do you think now?"

"I still think someone's playing you for a sucker."

Ortega's eyes narrowed. That did nothing to dim the glitter behind the squinting lids. Then his eyes opened and he waved an impatient hand to the four men gathered around me. "We waste time. Take him somewheres and get started."

They yanked me to my feet and spun me around. Two pairs of hands held me and jerked me forward. Someone behind me gave me a healthy kick in the rump. For reasons I was not keen about I began to imagine a picture of Vito having to go over my bruised remains, trying to figure out what had finished me off, that is if there was anything to find at all. It did not strike me as the most encouraging thought I had had so far.

A crash came from down below in the chop shop. The guys tugging me along did not let go, but they looked toward the windows. They had turned enough for me to see Ortega go over to the windows and look down to see what was causing the ruckus. I heard more crashes, then a shot.

A burst of machine gunfire echoed through the work area, the staccato chatter an Uzi makes. Then came the *thump, thump, thump* of a heavier caliber semiautomatic weapon set on single-fire. Ortega cursed in Spanish. I thought I heard a muffled scream below.

Ortega looked up and ducked back, but too late. A pair of boots crashed through the large pane of glass. A compact figure came through on the length of swinging chain, landed inside the window and rolled across the floor. Joz Brosche came up on one knee, a gun in one hand and her other hand going for another. She began to fire.

The hands holding me let go. One guy fell as dead weight to the floor. The other fellow dove toward the floor, flinching in mid-flight. He did not get up. The fellow who had kicked me fell down and was not going to get back up either.

Ortega stood at the desk, tugging at a drawer when a shot hit him in the right shoulder. He jerked back. The last fellow near me had a gun all the way out of his holster. I rushed to him, hit his elbow with my palm as he fired. The shot took out a neon light. Behind me I heard Ortega scream as he took another shot to his left elbow.

The fellow near me had his gun on the downward path. I reached and grabbed his wrist, then felt his whole body go limp. I had heard and felt the whiz past my ear. I looked him in the face, saw the third eye, the hole in his forehead.

"Joz," I said. She had turned to square off against Ortega, who had fallen back into his chair. He alternately cried out and cursed. Blood ran down both useless arms. Joz stayed in stance but slowly lowered the barrel of one pistol.

"Don't," I said. "You finish him off and this war may never end, no matter who started it."

The door behind me swung open and I spun. It was Cassie. She had an automatic weapon slung over her back, a pistol in her right hand. She shoved in another clip. "Come on, you guys. We've only got seconds." She had tied her hair back into a long ponytail. It whirled as she turned and fired at footsteps clambering up the metal stairs.

I turned back around to see Ortega struggle to his feet. His face clenched into an angry grimace. He lowered his head like a bull and charged. More and more the things he did impressed me less with his wisdom.

Joz stepped to one side, chopped his neck with a pistol as he went by. He veered and headed toward Cassie. Joz stuck out a leg and he tripped, fell to his left toward the glass. His shoulder hit first. With all that momentum he tumbled on through. His scream stopped abruptly when he hit the cement floor below.

"This is going well," I said.

"Come on," Cassie said again, and started down the stairs. Joz and I scrambled behind her, Joz covering the area. There was no one to shoot at us, whether they had left after seeing Ortega hit or because there were just no more of them, I could not tell.

As we started down the stairs I did see where the jack had been knocked away from the corner of one car. Legs stuck out from beneath it. They kicked hard as we started down the stairs, had slowed by the time we got to the bottom.

Cassie led the way out, another direction from the one where I had been brought in. No other men opposed us. I did spot one or two sprawled on the floor along the way we left. I had to guess at their status, but did not have much hope for them since Joz was along.

The getaway car was Joz's, beat-up, hunter green early '70s Land Cruiser. She had left it idling. We piled in, me in the back. Joz peeled out and we were off. I listened, but could hear no approaching sirens. The whole rescue must have happened in under five minutes. The part I had witnessed had taken less time than that.

"Thanks," I said, once we were out mingled in traffic and heading back to the center of town in as roundabout way as Joz could manage. Now I did hear a siren or two. "Don't you two get tired of rescuing me?"

"Probably 'bout as much as you get tired of bein' rescued," Joz said.

Cassie turned halfway around in her seat. "Where's your chubby redhead friend now?"

I ignored her question. "Jimmy tell you Ortega had me?"

"Yeah."

"How'd you know where they would take me?"

"We trailed 'em there a day ago. What were you doing hanging 'round a recording studio in the middle of all that's going on?"

I couldn't very well say I'd been dodging them, trying to find a place to stay where I could avoid them.

"How'd he know where to find you?"

"We've been staying at his house, in a tent in the backyard. It's raising holy hell with his girlfriend."

"I can imagine." I wondered why Jimmy had not told me, then figured his fear of Joz was greater than his friendship to me. Knowing Joz, I figured that to be a wise choice.

"You came out of all that with very little, except your own skin," Cassie said.

"I did find out earlier where the other faction of illegals is camped." I gave them the coordinates I had gotten at the hospital. "Where are you taking me?"

"To your place," Joz said. "You know, the one you're never at."

"When did you two quit staying there?"

"We just decided to find other digs."

"Why? Did you see Borster, half the INS, maybe a couple of detectives named Barnett and Kilgallon?"

"I never saw anyone like you for attracting a crowd. It made coming and going a real challenge."

"So why do we now *want* to be seen there?"

"Right now an alibi wouldn't hurt you any," Cassie said.

"You think if I come in all sweaty, with a car left behind on a sidewalk, and with a few battle scars, no one will think I was in a fight?"

"What happened to your face?"

"I was trying to help someone give up smoking."

Joz said, "My guess is that the local law will be drawn to Ortega's place like flying bugs to a nightlight. Maybe the INS too. That should give you time to get inside and settle."

"You're probably right."

"You know I am. Remember," Joz said, "you heard it here first on Roller Derby."

I got out of the shower and wandered nude out to my desk. Earlier I had spotted what was left of a bottle of tequila there. What with one thing and another in this case I had been knocked off my drinking. I poured a small dose and was taking a sip when I heard a knock at the door.

"Just a minute." I washed back the rest of what was in the glass and scrambled for my clothes. I wondered which of them it would be. When I had on pants and shirt, though no shoes and tie, I peeked through the peephole, then swung the door open.

L. Leroy Hunt stormed into my small office as if expecting it to be the foyer to a bigger place. He stopped abruptly when he realized that he looked at all there was to the place, unless he wanted to go into the small back room where I slept.

"I can't believe you live like this."

I poured myself another half inch of refreshment, sat on the corner of my desk and knocked it back. "I'm sure you didn't come to discuss my accommodations. What brings you here?"

He stared at the bottle on the desk. I shrugged, reached across and pulled a drawer open enough to pull out another sample of my fine crystal. This drinking glass was also one of my empty dried-beef jars. They are sturdy and functional, though not likely to help me climb any social ladders.

I poured him an inch and held out the glass. He took it with a hand that had a visible tremor. He had left his shirt open at the collar, the tie loosened. Still, he wore first class threads. I had to wonder about him. One minute he's stonewalling and threatening to throw me out of his office, the next we are chums having a social moment.

He drank from his glass, continued to look around the room in some wonder. There wasn't much to see. The walls didn't have so much as a calendar on them. There was room for the desk, a couple of chairs, and not a whole lot more. This was a hard visit for him. He seemed to wrestle with being in control versus getting to the subject of whatever bugged him. I let him take his own pace. "I don't quite get you," he said. "What's your motivation?"

"What do you mean?"

"You live like this, have one worn suit that could stand dry cleaning. I mean, why do you do what you do?"

I suppose he might have understood if it was something as simple as money. I felt no need to try to explain myself to someone like him. "Why the visit?" I tried again.

"I wasn't myself before," he said. His eyes flickered away from mine. Something was sure under his skin. "I might've been a little hasty, harsh."

"Do you think?"

"Oh, take a jab at me if you think I need it, and I probably do. I can get a little rough."

"You the one who put the bruises on Lola's arms?"

He swallowed, hesitated, then said, "I might have handled Lola a bit rough. In fairness, she gave back as much as she got. I could show *you* a few bruises."

"Spare me."

"I mean it. She started most of the brawls. Something was bothering her. At the same time, I can't say when her music was ever better. I don't mean just what she sang in the club there, but what she was writing on her own. She sure seemed inspired, cranking out song after song. But she had never been as miserable either. I guess I'm not making a whole lot of sense."

"You came here to tell me that?"

"No. That'd mean I care what you think about me, and I don't. All I care about is finding whoever did what they did to Lola."

"I have a client."

"I'll pay you more." That must have meant a lot, coming from someone as tight as he was.

"It's not up for bid."

He lifted the fingers of his right hand to his forehead, rubbed the fingers back and forth before catching himself and lowering the hand. "Can I hire you for something else?"

"What?"

"Someone's making harassing calls. I answer and it's Lola's voice."

"Call the phone company," I said. "Or get caller ID. I don't chase ghosts."

"You'll at least let me know what you find?"

I stared at him, surprised a businessman like him could even suggest that.

Someone knocked at the door. His head snapped that way in a nervous jerk. I got up off the desk and went and opened the door. A big man in a dark expensive suit stood looking past me into my office. I had never seen him before.

He nodded back to two men who leaned against a black limo at the curb. When his head panned back toward me he looked past me into the office. He ignored me, spoke to Hunt. "Not another word."

I glanced at him, then the limo. So, this was Jake Hunger. I might have been part of the door frame for all the attention he paid to me. Hard to believe this was an elected official given all the personality he shared. Hunt came to the door and pushed his way past. He headed for his car, a Jaguar parked in front of the limo.

The hardest thing for me to take was seeing a man let another take his balls that way, all for money. I doubted if I would ever be able to look Hunt in the eyes again.

Jake Hunger looked at me for the first time. Our eyes were on a level, but he had a knack for looking down at me. The first words he ever shared with me were, "If you so much as tell a peep of anything he said, I will do whatever I have to do to ruin you in this town. Understood?"

Hunger spun on his heel and headed off toward the limo without another word. My friend Lori had hinted that he had bought most of his votes, which I began to believe.

As for L. Leroy Hunt, he was a complex person. I had caught phases of his personality from half a dozen angles and hadn't liked any of them. Perhaps he paid his price in life by being around someone like Jake Hunger.

The caravan pulled out. It had started to get hot outside. I went back inside, where it was not a whole lot cooler, and closed the door. I had gotten my shoes on and had started to put on my tie when another knock came at the door. I did not even look out the peephole this time. There was no way this visit could make less sense than the last one.

Len Jacobus and Miles stood there in the heat. I finished tying my tie before waving them inside.

"You know," Jacobus said, giving my office the same eye of appreciation that Hunt had given it, "we once had a pretty fair idea of what was going on in this town. But dating almost from the point that you got involved, we know less than we ever did. Do you have a feeling for what is going on?"

"In respect to what?" I said. I watched Miles, didn't expect much of a response from Jacobus. Miles started to grin, then caught Jacobus's face swinging his way.

"Did you know that Ortega is dead?"

"When did that happen?" I said. "Doesn't that simplify things for you?"

"Just a while ago. And no, it doesn't. We knew he was tied to coyotes bringing in illegals. But we didn't have anything to pin on him. Nor do we know who he was working for. We were getting closer, though. Now we have to start over."

"I'm surprised you have time to take from such a busy investigation to visit me."

"We think you're more involved than you let on."

"That right? And then what, I'm supposed to just tell you stuff?"

Jacobus wasn't a good investigator. Miles and I knew it, but we were the only ones in the room who did. Jacobus's instincts may have been fine. Yet he lacked the mental toolkit to do more than prod at a case, pick at it like a scab. He had none of the silent but deadly qualities I ascribe to his counterparts in the FBI.

"If I can find some way to smear you in the course of this investigation, I think you should know that I plan to do so," he said.

It seemed I had my share of well-wishers today. This charming interchange got interrupted by the door opening. No knock this time. There stood my close and personal friends, Barnett and Kilgallon.

"Turn on your TV," Kilgallon said. "There's something you should see."

He and Barnett looked around the room, saw no television, not even a radio. They did spot Jacobus and Miles, though.

"Sound like the next Hispanic civil war?" Jacobus asked.

"Worse than that." Barnett glared at me. "There's been a leak somewhere that ties everything into one wrinkled-ass mess.

The story of the moment, the recent mayhem at Ortega's place aside, is back to putting the spotlight on vampires."

"This is just the kind of thing I was talking about." He slammed the folded newspaper onto the desk.

"We can't control the reporters."

"Where did they get this?"

"Not from our people."

"You think our vampire called in? Didn't think he was getting his share of the spotlight anymore?"

"He might have if he's trying to muddy the waters."

"Muddy or not, you know what this means?"

"What, Captain?"

"The clock is ticking. That sense of urgency you can feel like a boot up your butt is now official."

CHAPTER SEVENTEEN

"What happened to your cheek?" Barnett looked at the Band-Aid I had applied after my shower. "And don't say you cut yourself shaving."

"Okay," I said. "I won't."

"You know, going smart-mouth on us isn't going to help you any." Kilgallon glared. "We're going to need someone to fall for this, and soon. If it comes to it, you might do in a pinch."

"You can pretend you didn't hear that," I told Jacobus. He had been watching the exchange so far with a wrinkled forehead. Miles seemed to be enjoying it, but was as prone to speak as ever.

"Why is it so hard for you to just shoot straight with us?" Barnett asked.

"Fellows," Jacobus said.

I had heard so much about Barnett and Kilgallon, what a crack homicide team they were, that I had thought they might be different, from, say, Borster. My recent visit from Jake Hunger had made me aware he was a man who could buy people, cops included. To the moment, I had no indication that Barnett and Kilgallon weren't in his pocket. Not that I am ever chatty about a case, but the added element of Jake Hunger to the case did nothing to encourage me. He had thrown everything into an even more deadly and uncertain light.

"If you think we were getting a hotfoot before," Barnett said to Jacobus, "you can imagine what it's like now with this vampire scare back bigger than ever on top of a Hispanic power struggle that's turned into a war."

"I understand where you're coming from," Jacobus cast a wary eye toward me, not comfortable speaking candidly in front of me, "but we still do have rank as the Federal agents here. We get to speak with him first."

Kilgallon spun to me. "I suppose you claim you don't know anything about what happened to Ortega."

"Agent Jacobus here was just bringing me up to speed on Ortega," I said.

"Don't try to squirm out." Kilgallon wouldn't let it go. "You were seen being taken from your car by Hispanics. The next thing we hear Ortega's place is a battleground you wouldn't believe to look at it."

"No kidding?"

"You really don't have much to hold him on," Jacobus said, "hardly even material witness. You're working with second and third source conjecture and rumor."

"You stay out of this," Barnett said.

"Maybe we should . . ." Whatever Jacobus was going to say got interrupted by the phone. All four of them looked at me. I reached for it.

"Is Cassie there with you?" It was Joz.

"No. Why?"

"I left her watching the other Los Olvidados camp for an hour. Now she's not there."

"Do you—?" I did not get to ask if Joz thought she had been snatched. Joz had hung up.

Jacobus and Barnett glared at each other. Both looked just short of rolling up their sleeves.

"Why don't you step outside for a moment while we discuss this?" Barnett did not look at me while he spoke, his eyes stayed locked with those of the INS agent.

"Miles, go with him and keep an eye on him."

Still sitting on the desk, I shrugged, reached and lifted the bottle to my mouth. I tilted it up, but kept my tongue over the end. I didn't crave a drink, but I wanted them to think I did. Nothing puts an authority figure more off his guard than thinking your powers are under a cloud and his are not.

I stood and walked to the door, flipped the latch as I went out. When Miles came out behind me the dead-bolt lock kept the door from closing. He had to turn and flip the inside toggle of the lock.

Shadows stretched all the way across the street. The sun teetered on the lip of the horizon. It would be dark very soon.

His back was to me. I hated to do it to Miles, who until this point had been the most benign of them. I cut into a soft-step Indian-like run the minute his back was turned. I shot around the corner and headed for the back of the building before he could have fixed the lock.

Around back, where I sometimes park my car when I know where it is, a rusty fire escape ladder hung frozen in place. I leaped and caught the bottom rung, pulled myself up hand-over-hand until I could get my feet in the rungs. Then I scampered quietly up the rest of the way, expecting to hear running steps in the gravel below at any time.

At the top I flipped up over onto the roof. The tar surface was hot and sticky. But someone had put a row of boards along the edge to walk on. I stayed low and eased around to the front of the building. I heard shouting below.

Barnett ran to the left on the sidewalk, Kilgallon to the right. Jacobus screamed at Miles as they walked back to the dead end of the alley that doglegged behind the building, then came to a stop against a sheer brick wall. Some time back I had tracked a murderer by spotting flakes of rust in the gravel below the ladder and following a trail that led up the fire escape. Neither of them had much in the way of tracking abilities. They walked back up the alley to the street to wait on Barnett and Kilgallon.

The sun had gone the rest of the way down and it was darker when the detectives came down the street together from the right. They had met somewhere on the other side of the block before giving up the chase. I ducked back behind the edge and could not catch all of the conversation that followed. The tone suggested a hint of anger on both sides.

It took another twenty minutes for them to sort out their differences before getting into their cars and pulling away. I watched to make sure they all got in.

When they were gone I climbed down off the building. I didn't even take time to lock up my office, didn't trust them not to leave someone watching the door for a while. In the darkening streets I crept off between parked cars until I was a block away. Then I began a slow trot toward the nearest hotel, where I knew I had a better chance of catching a cab.

A red and key lime green Roy's Taxi dropped me off at the corner where I'd been abducted. Someone had bothered to drive the silver Volvo off the sidewalk and park it in a parking slot, where it now had a couple of yellow tickets under the left wiper. The door was unlocked and the keys still in the dash, which gives some idea of how badly people crave stealing Volvos.

It grew dark as I got in, turned on the lights, and drove away. The chances that my pals had an APB out on me seemed slim. Though I suspected that if they spotted me on their own, they would be after me in a flash. The tickets fluttered on the windshield until I unrolled the window, reached out and grabbed them, shoved them into the glove box. I soon headed out Manor Road, due east from the center of Austin through the middle of what the police call Charlie Sector.

The battle lines between the unwitting illegal alien camps reflected some of the same turf issues that affected Austin's embryonic gangs. The illegals, who had been aligned with Ortega, had been from Frank Sector, or Southeast Austin. The coordinates Estaban's mother had shared were off to the east, but farther north, behind a flea market and not far from the Manor Downs race track.

The lights of the city faded behind me. I made a left turn onto a smaller road, went down the prescribed two miles, turned left again. When I got close, I slowed the car, pulled over and eased the car off the road until I could ease it behind a long shed where in season firecrackers were sold. The car was half hidden from the other direction by a chinaberry tree.

I stayed close to a wooden fence. Then I had to slip over three strands of barbed wire, duck low, and sprint across an open field to a row of sumac bushes and mesquite that ran along the edge of the next property. The closer I got, the more noise and music I heard. I heard chatter in Spanish, most of it far faster than I could handle. But I had not come here to listen.

I moved slowly around the perimeter of the camp, looked in when I could to see if I spotted Cassie. Small fires burned in front of tents and wooden sheds. The area looked like the site of a run-down house and barn, what was left of a small ranch. The group, or someone on their behalf, may have bought it. Or they could be squatting. It took some time just to get around the outside of the gathering. There seemed to be quite a few of them in there. I caught scratchy radio versions of *norteño* ballads. Other people sang from their firesides, the sound of their guitars carrying farther than the songs.

It seemed a shame that these two camps could not hear each other at night, see how similar they were. It might help them get along instead of being driven into whatever conflict those steering them had created.

A dark suit is a fine thing for creeping around at night except for the little forms of vegetation that want to climb on for the ride. I stopped where a thread of flickering light from one of the fires fell on me. I picked flat white threads of seeds and round sandy-colored burrs from my socks and the bottom of my slacks.

A rustle behind me made me look up. I saw the leveled gun, then saw that it was held by Joz. She lowered the gun. "What the hell're you doing?" she whispered.

"Came looking for Cassie."

She pushed the rest of the way out of the bush and moved closer enough to speak softly. "I don't know what that woman has, but I should bottle it and sell it. Every nutcase in Texas seems to go after her with his tongue hanging out, you included. That ought to be worth something."

"Why do you care so much about money?" I meant, hadn't she done very well, thank you, with the cash she made off with when she took the paramilitary's treasury less than a year ago. I didn't say that.

"It's just the way I am," she said, which pretty much settled that.

"You haven't seen her, have you?"

"No."

"Where was she last?"

"We split up to search the camp. She started around one way. I took the other. We were supposed to meet on the other side. I've been back through half a dozen times, covering all the angles. I haven't found her, and there's very few places one could hide, or be hidden."

"What were you looking for in the first place?"

"I'd still be in there checking, but those goons arrived."

"What goons?" I said. "And you dodged a question."

"Tall guys in black, about a dozen of them."

While we had whispered, all the radios and guitars had

stopped in the camp. "What makes you think something happened to her?"

"Where we were to meet, I found her gun, kicked or tossed under a bush."

I didn't, *couldn't* say anything.

"That's when I went back and forth through the camp again. It's no worse than a gypsy camp, except for those guys who just arrived."

"It was the money," I said. "You two thought you could find that here. Why?"

"We got into Levi's house, searched it from one end to the other. Found nothing there."

I looked through the bushes over toward the camp. A crowd had gathered at the center. The outskirts were deserted. "Let's go," I said.

The two of us eased through the other side of the bushes into the edge of the camp. I heard a single voice speaking in a repetitive tone, building into something like a chant. We didn't want to go too close. So we hung back as soon as we were near enough to tell what was happening. Joz disappeared into the shadow of a tent flap. I tucked myself behind a partially tumbled cement-block silo. There was enough of it standing for me to peer through an inch-wide crack without being seen.

Levi stood on a raised spot with his tall men in black gathered on either side like wings. He wore all black, and a cape. His face looked unusually pale in the light from a few lanterns and campfires.

What words I could make out were gibberish, some in Latin, others Spanish. It seemed mumbo-jumbo of the mumbo-jumbiest sort. I panned what faces in the crowd I could see.

Some were rapt, others merely looked Levi's way, as if aware of who handed out the pay envelopes. It appeared that Levi's days as an acolyte were not wasted. The rite he was going through seemed little more than a perversion of a Catholic mass.

His arms lifted, the black cape spreading, each side lifting like wings. In the dim light and flickering fires he sure enough looked the part of a giant bat with a ghoulish long face about to lift and hover above them. His voice droned and voices in the crowd picked up the litany. If ever he seemed to be the Prince of Darkness he did now, to me and so to many of those assembled here.

I looked through the crowd for any sign of Cassie, not paying too much attention to what Levi said until I caught a sentence in English that even I could understand. He told them they needed to disband for a while, scatter into other places until Austin calmed down. Some of those present had to be the people he had sent against the wrecking yard. His advice did not seem all that out of line.

Shooting broke out on two fronts at the other side of the camp. Levi dropped down from his raised position and the tall men in black gathered around him as they took off through the crowd. People ran in all directions. I spun and headed back the way we had come. Joz was already on the move and setting a pace ahead of me.

Machine gunfire stuttered, coming in from several directions now. Some of the men had gotten to their tents and were returning fire. I could hear screams from children and women above the guns. The loud whump of a grenade going off was too close for my comfort. I picked up the pace and caught up with Joz. She ran with a gun in either hand and glanced around her the whole time, though the attack seemed to be from other directions. We stepped lively all the way to my car. She climbed into the passenger seat.

"Forget my car," she said. "It's out of the way. We hiked a ways in to the camp. Let's get the hell oughta here."

"You didn't see Cassie anywhere in all that?" I asked, putting the key in the ignition. I had the window down, could hear an explosion, then another. We sat out of range from the screaming. A breathy saxophone played in a far corner of my head, its notes climbing and dropping, lifting back into a wail.

"No. I didn't. Wherever she is, she's on her own for the moment."

I sat in the driver's seat, but didn't turn the key.

"What are you waiting for, Trav?"

"I can't leave."

"Why?"

"I'm going back and do what I can about the women and kids."

"Are you nuts? It's a war back there."

"You picked up Cassie's gun, you said. Do you still have it?"

She reached back and pulled an automatic out from where she had shoved it under her belt at the small of her back. "You don't even like guns. You *never* carry one."

"I'm not too ripped about having one with me now. But I may need it if I'm going back into that."

She sighed. "I begin to see what there is about you that bugged Cassie."

I got out of the car, left the keys in the ignition. "Take off if you want. I'll find some other way back."

"Oh, hell." She took the keys out and tossed them to me. "Let's go. You're gonna need someone at your back."

L. Leroy Hunt turned off the lights and got out of his Chrysler. The first place he had found open in the extended-stay lot had been in the third row from the back. He had left the Jaguar back in the garage. The shuttle bus went past. There would not be another one for fifteen minutes. "Damn."

He got his one bag out of the trunk, walked across the dark lot to the lighted glass enclosure to wait on the next shuttle. He had electronic tickets. That would make up any time he lost. He did not like waiting here in the asshole end of the lot this late.

A scratch of gravel and the click of a step turned his head.

"Oh. It's you."

"We all have to travel. Lot cheaper to park way out here, isn't it?"

Hunt made a soft grunt. That was the last they spoke.

The sky was black. No stars were showing. He looked down, saw the end of a folded piece of money. He took a half step forward until one shoe covered the bill, then bent forward to tie a shoe. It was a twenty.

Whatever hit his head was hard and unforgiving. He was out long before his unconscious body fell over onto the asphalt. But it didn't hurt. Nothing was ever going to hurt again.

CHAPTER EIGHTEEN

We ran back to the camp until we flitted from building to tent, staying low, cutting through low clouds of smoke. I shoved Cassie's pistol into my suit jacket as I ran, not real comfortable with trying to save women and kids while waving a gun around. The idea did not bother Joz, who leaped over the body of a fallen man in a black suit and cape.

Considerable screaming came from ahead to our right. As we got closer I slowed. The bulk of the women, children way ahead of them, tried to squeeze through a gap in a tall wooden fence all at once as they got away from the heart of the fighting.

Back to my left I could see a small cluster of heads huddled behind an overturned table. "Joz." When she stopped and came back to me, I said, "Looks like the others are fine. They're getting out. There's a handful pinned down back here."

A spray of automatic weapon fire made us both dive for cover. We scrambled forward on hands and knees. I looked around, but couldn't see that we were the target. There seemed to be a lot of random shooting going on. Three men, shooting as they ran, went by in the smoke to our right and didn't see us. An explosion went off taking out a tent to our rear. I couldn't tell if someone was working a howitzer or throwing grenades. The explosion left a ringing in my ears that made it harder to hear the shouting and screaming going on all around us.

I dragged myself through the racket, dust, and smoke to the overturned table. One of the men had been trying to cover for the four women huddled there, but he lay at one end of the table, fallen across his automatic weapon. Each of the women held a baby. It's what had kept them from keeping up with the others. Each mother had wide eyes in a tear-streamed face. They looked at me with mixed fear and relief. It must have been the dark suit. Seeing Joz comforted them, even when she was busy scooping up the automatic weapon. We gathered the women and got them moving, led them toward the car in as straight a path as random fires, collapsed tents, and the continued shooting would let us.

Once we got to the edge of the camp we made better time. Joz turned and shot at the only people to see us making our getaway. Then the bunch of us hurried on to the car. All four women and their babies piled into the backseat. Most of the babies and a couple of the mothers still cried very loud. Joz rolled down her window as I drove out from where I'd hid the car. The flash of gunshots lit up the road ahead of us. I spun the car around and headed east, would have to take the long way around to get back to Austin. In the far distance I heard sirens approaching, all coming from the direction of the city far behind us.

A car pulled out and pursued. It began to gain on us. Someone leaned out from the passenger side to fire toward us.

"Who's shooting at us," I said, "Ortega's men or Levi's?"

"Does it matter?"

Joz climbed halfway out her window and turned back to spray the car behind us. She fired until the automatic weapon clicked on empty. Then she tossed it aside out the window, pulled out one of her pistols.

I watched through the rearview window, saw the car swerve then veer off to the left. It ran across the median and the opposing lanes, sparks flew from the rim where its tire had been shot flat. The car disappeared as I kept the gas to floor.

The dark of night began to be a comfort to us. I turned right when I could and took back roads heading south around Lake Long before I turned the car and headed back toward Austin.

The crying in the backseat settled down to soft weeping by one of the women. All of the babies and two of the women had fallen asleep.

"What do you plan to do with our passengers?" Joz asked as the city lights got brighter.

"I'll think of something." Fifteen minutes later I pulled up beside the Catholic church.

Late as it was, Sister Consuela and a few other nuns came out to help the women and their babies into the church.

Sister Consuela looked over at Joz, who leaned against the car, then at me. "Do I need to know what is going on?"

"I don't think so. Probably better if you don't know."

"Good," she said. "I do not understand the fighting. There should be no they; only us."

"I think most of the ones doing the fighting are just as confused," I said. "Let's hope it's nearly over."

"Nearly?" she said. Before I could respond, she added, "Everything is relative. If you were on the sun you'd weigh two tons."

Joz pushed away from the side of the car and opened her door as I got to it. "What was that all about?"

"Don't make me try to explain Sister Consuela." I started the car and pulled out. It had gotten late, but not so late that I felt it was safe for me to go back to my office. I said, "You still staying at Bravuro's place?"

"Where else?"

"*My* friend Jimmy Bravuro," I said.

"Think about it, Trav. Who would scare you more—you, or me?"

"Point taken."

I dropped her off in front of his place, waited until she had checked and found that Cassie wasn't there. Neither was Jimmy at the moment. She turned to go inside.

"Hey," I called out.

"What?"

I held out Cassie's gun.

"You don't think you'll need it?"

"You know I don't carry. And if we find Cassie, she may want it."

"If," she said, in a way I tried not to think about.

I couldn't very well go home to my office. As Joz said, there could be a stakeout from any number of factions. I suspected both the cops and the INS were higher on the list now that I had skipped out of out last little meeting.

The parking garage of the Marriott Hotel was a short walk from the forensics lab. I parked the car at the hotel and went to see my friend Vito.

The streets were dark—nothing to hear but the click of my steps. In a far corner of my head the low notes of that solo saxophone was breathing soft notes of some tune that sounded familiar, maybe one of Lola's songs. My back felt sore, my arms tired, and my suit was about a half step from belonging in a Goodwill bag. I wouldn't have said no to a drink had one been offered.

There was all kinds of excitement in Forensics. Bodies were piled up at the door on gurneys. Cops came and went. In the nearest thing to pass for a lull, I slipped through the metal doors and walked over to Vito. He stood over by the door of his office, not doing any autopsies at the second. Directing traffic and handling the incoming had to take most of his effort.

He saw me weave past a departing pair of EMS workers. "Oh, this figures. Tell me you don't have anything to do with all this." He waved an arm to the room. "They're taking some of them to hospitals, gonna do a few at County. But I'm looking at a week's worth of work before morning."

I held up a hand to stop the tirade. In the hand I had two packs of cigarettes, his brand. "In your office?" I said.

He reached and took the cigarettes, followed me inside. "Aha. Trying to kill me slowly, eh? Quick thinking. That could work." He tore the wrapper off a pack. "You are a saint, Trav. If ever I could stand a smoke, it's now."

He closed the door behind us.

I nodded toward the door. "You're sure getting business on the wholesale plan. What's up?"

"All hell broke out. It's not real forensics work. They don't need a pathologist for this. All we're trying to do is match bodies with weapons found, and that won't even tell us much. Looks like two factions having at each other."

"Including the men in black suits?"

"How'd you know about them?"

"Just saw one lying out there."

"You notice someone took the bother to drive a wooden stake through his heart, even though he was already dead?"

"So the media's going to get to scream 'vampire' some more."

He dug through his desk, found a book of matches and lit up. He looked out from under the cloud of smoke at me, his head tilted low enough to give me the angle of one eye.

"*Is* any of this your doing?"

"You know me, Vito. I don't even carry a gun. They don't need you out there in the lab?"

"No. We have every assistant and part-timer called in to do tagging and sort through the other reports. This one is going to take a while. Anything else you want to know?"

"Yeah. How's Lilian?"

He lowered the cigarette he had just lifted to his face. He

stared at me. "I didn't know you knew my wife."

"We don't run in the same social circles, eh? You're right. I've just heard of her. I ran into your father-in-law."

"That right? And he is?"

"Jake Hunger. How long did you think it would take me to make that connection? And more to the point, why didn't you give it to me in the first place?"

"I think you know why, if you've met Jake."

"How is he connected?"

"To what's going on? To all that you saw going on out there?" Vito nodded toward where the new arrivals were pouring in. He lit another cigarette off the stub of the one he had going.

"He was backing Ortega somehow, wasn't he?"

Vito shrugged, too elaborately.

"You can't prove it, but you thought it." I sat in my chair, exhausted, too tired to tilt the chair back. I slumped and watched Vito smoke, wished I had brought something to drink. "How does that link up with the vampire angle?"

He started to shrug, couldn't even get himself that far. "I'll tell you. I'm just about sick of reporters calling to ask if any bodies here are uncorrupted—that's supposed to mean not naturally decaying, a sign of someone who will become a vampire. It's like some macabre Halloween bad joke. Yet people are drooling over the story. And worse, there are people out there believing the story and in the early stages of panic. It's what I feared would happen all along."

"Well, they didn't get it from me. Any idea who keeps fueling the vampire story?"

"Oh, that's another sweetheart aspect of the deal. I got Homicide down here busting my chops about have I told anyone about the neck holes, any of that."

"I know. If I could have solved all this earlier, it's a bullet you could have dodged."

"I'm not blaming you, Trav. But the whole thing has turned into something much bigger and worse. By the way, when I last saw your pals, Detectives Barnett and Kilgallon, they were looking for you. What's that about?"

"I wouldn't worry about it—probably want to get the name of my decorator."

"No doubt."

"What's in all this for you?" I said.

He looked down, then up at me slowly, his jaw slipping to full jut. "Think carefully about my last name."

"Did you get the jutting jaw trick from your father or your mother's side?"

"What?"

"Nothing."

"My heritage almost kept us from getting married. Jake was not keen about having his daughter marry a Hispanic."

"But he doesn't mind exploiting the illegals, do you think?" I said.

"Putting aside the issue of Jake Hunger's involvement, or whether I ever get laid at home again or not, we still have a war on our hands."

"Only as long as there's leadership. And Ortega's dead, isn't he?"

"Did him already, and yes, he seemed dead enough. Your work?"

"And there's this Levi on the other side, who is also our top candidate in the vampire department. It seems pretty transparent that he's behind scaring his faction of illegals into robberies and who knows what else with all that Prince of Darkness crap. His hand is on the table now. He's got to be, what, twenty-six or twenty-seven—an intense fellow, with the mental powers of a much younger man. His little get-rich turn at entrepreneurship is about to be over. Do you think all this will just die down?"

Vito eyed the open pack of smokes on his desk. He had just rubbed another butt out after going through that cancer stick in record time. "Oh, what the hell," he said. He reached for the pack again.

"They don't kill you all in one night," I said.

"Too bad." He lighted up. The lit end bobbed, the cigarette hung from the corner of his mouth, as he said, "You know that the police department is in the process of decentralizing. Soon, each of the half-dozen sectors will have its own unit. Your two hottest ones will be Frank Sector, Southeast Austin, where Ortega's people were focused, and Charlie Sector, the one just above that, East Austin, where the people in tonight's night dance are centered. They're the ones Levi probably controlled."

"I know about the sectors. And?"

"What gang activity Austin has, and any city this size has a dose, is in the same two sectors. And we have the full range. There're Bloods, Brothas, Crips, Latin Kings, Los Cholos, Outlawz, and half a dozen other color-wearing crews. Almost fifty percent of all arrests in those two sectors are of Hispanics. And thirty-five percent of all victims are Hispanic."

"I know about the gangs. Didn't that organized narcotics bust, Big Dawg, snag a few?"

"Mostly Outlawz, known as OZs. My point's that very few of the illegals have any gang ties. They were outside all that."

"So, you have a new segment of population to exploit and get rich from. Right?"

"And someone was doing just that. Looks like Levi's whole wealth came from this, the opportunistic bastard."

"How come they haven't just brought him in?"

"On what grounds—that he thinks he's a vampire, or the devil? All you have is suspicion and conjecture, and that's just between us. I think we're a step or two ahead in our thinking of where the law is. Facing the vampire thing has been a big speed bump for them, one they would have gladly swept under the rug before letting the public panic."

"As the public is doing. Hell, the paper's back to giving more play to one or two deaths like that than all of these men, even women and a child or two in the recent battles."

"Hollywood's done that for you."

There was a knock on the door. We shut up. "What?" Vito said.

"Couple of cops here to see you."

"Tell 'em to get in line."

"They say it can't wait, sir. They're bringing in someone who they want moved to the front of the line."

Vito jumped to his feet, reached and twisted the cigarette out in the tray. "Just who the hell . . . ?"

"It's some guy named Hunt—L. Leroy Hunt."

"Tell 'em I'll be right out." Vito reached and turned out the light. "Will you be all right in here?"

I reached below the desk to tug out the rolled sleeping bag. "It's the best offer I've had for a place to stay all night," I said.

Friends all forsake you, leave you stuck in the mire,
Share everything with you, except the dark fire.

CHAPTER NINETEEN

First thing in the morning, a bleary-eyed Vito turned me and my rumpled suit loose on the world. I went to a phone and made a long-distance call to West Texas. Sheriff Harmon Cuthers was in, though it took a moment or two for him to come onto the phone. I stretched while standing beside the phone booth. The sun was already giving the thermometer a hotfoot. Today would be a scorcher. I felt, if anything, more stiff and sore than when I had collapsed on Vito's floor for the night.

"Yeah," Harmon's voice came on the line. "Get talkin'. It's your dime."

"It's Travis here. Do you remember me?"

"I'm getting on. But I'm not senile yet." Harmon was in his mid-sixties, not too uncommon for a sheriff of a small county of forty thousand people.

"I'm calling about Cassie."

"What about her?"

"She was here in Austin, helping look into a case."

"I know that. It's *her* vacation time. I could've picked better ways to spend it."

"She hasn't showed up around there, has she?"

"No. Why would she?"

"I thought she might have gone back there to see the new deputy she's dating."

"The only new deputy we have here is Hazel, who you met, and Cassie sure as boot spit isn't dating him. Who handed you

233

that load of cow manure?"

"Just checking."

"Don't you have any crime wave or anything to fight there in the city, or anything else to keep you busy? From what I'm hearing in the news the gates of hell've opened up over there."

It was still an hour or two before most people have breakfast when I knocked on the cottage door. It took a couple of hearty turns of knocking before the peephole darkened. Then the door swung open. Eva stood there in a robe over a nightgown looking not a bit like anyone called Madam Rostini. She looked like Mae West, with tousled red curly hair and bedroom eyes.

"Well, now, aren't you a sight to make the eyes sore? Did you lose your razor *and* your dry cleaner? Oh, come on in."

The inside of her cottage felt cooler and more cozy than the outside. She turned and seemed very close to me. I took a step back.

"Don't be so shy."

"I'm not," I said, felt myself run into the table behind me.

"Can't you tell I've been dieting just for you?"

"But what . . . ?" I looked at the big eyes in the pretty face, all moving too close to me. I eased around the table, keeping some distance between us.

"You knew I was interested, and it was fated. You were such an empty shell—just right for a relationship. Do you want to see . . . ?" Her hand went to the belt of her robe.

"No."

Her eyes had a hurt look, but the hand at her belt stopped undoing the knot.

"You should know that I like people with an appetite for life, however it's manifested. It's my vicarious lifeline."

She stared at me, blank faced, a single tear running in a trail down her round perfect cheek.

"I'm no expert on this," I said. "But any changes you make for anyone other than yourself are only going to make you resent that person more if things don't work out. And they usually don't."

"Well, Ann Landers you ain't," she said.

I nodded. "This I have realized before. I get a refresher course every now and then." I was thinking of Cassie, about what little good I am at any kind of a relationship beyond casual friendship. "I know I want to make some small difference, but it's never going to be by complementing someone else's life, or giving the world children. So I've had to struggle to find other ways to matter."

"That's some fancy rationalization."

"I wish it was. It's taken me too long and a few bumps to get to that, and it's only just becoming clear to me."

"But why come to me? What did you . . . ?"

"I need your help." She was some fortune-teller, I thought, but kept that to myself.

"There's nothing I can . . ."

"When did Lola come to you about the intravenous device?"

That rocked her back. Her flushed face went pale. "What do you . . . ? How . . . ?"

"Don't say there wasn't one. Lola went off the rails. I think that's what pushed her. She got her hands on the damned thing. She'd been wrestling with her conscience for some time. It's like you said, she probably got herself worked up to the point she really believed she had sold her soul to the devil. Getting her hands on the device Levi used on a couple of Ortega's people must have popped the bubble. Once she knew she'd been spoofed she had to make things right. She used her own money, I figure, to pay back the amount she knew had been taken from the Catholic church you all attended."

Eva moved back from me as if I held some flaming cross.

I said, "It's one thing to think you can sell your soul to the devil. It's another when you find that the devil isn't a very nice fellow at all. Levi was willing to cross any barriers, family, church. Nothing mattered to him. He even went to the elaborate trouble of rigging a doppelganger, Lila, to keep Lola off balance. I mean, I can't think of anything lower—finding a person's worst fear and going out of your way to use it to control them. And it worked on Lola, for a while. Getting the device made the whole thing a fraud. It took something like that, something she could hold and see, and know Levi for the fake he is, to make her snap, for her to become a liability."

"What device are you . . . ?"

"It would have a vacuum pump, a couple of blunt tooth-sized needles—the kind of thing you could shove in someone's neck and draw out blood, lots of it, too much of it."

"Have you seen such a . . . ?"

"I don't have to. I think Levi had it, probably made it. He used it as part of his scare tactics with the illegal aliens. He knew how superstitious they can be, had probably picked that up with the games he played in school. Lola got her hands on the damned thing. There had been victims before, and they have started up again. You read the papers, watch the news, don't you?"

"What's all that have to do with Lola? She's . . . she's dead." Her face turned away and she stared at the wall.

"No, I'm not saying she's around as a vampire, though the media would love that spin."

"How do you know she had this . . . this device?"

"I don't know for stone-cold sure. It's just the only way the thing makes sense. Something gave her the reality slap, and it had to be something concrete, and shocking. The other thing is that the nature of victims shifted. Someone took the damn thing from Lola. Instead of illegal aliens from a competing group the victims were people who knew Lola well. Almost everyone she could have told is dead now, except you."

"You don't think . . . ?"

"Whoever is doing the killing either doesn't know about you, or thinks you won't talk anyway, or just hasn't gotten to you yet."

Eva made a swallowed gasp. Her face still turned away from me. "The poor thing must have been living a hell."

I said, "The irony is that the anguish was making her sing and write better than ever. My own opinion is that writing the songs was her salvation, and the cause of her death. They helped her see clearly. They were her therapy. And that wasn't what someone wanted."

"You think . . . Levi?"

"Why don't you tell me the part you've saved?"

She turned back to me. Her pretty face was smeared with tears. I put my hands on her shoulders. They were soft and nice shoulders. She moved close and I let her. She pressed against me. All of her was soft and nice, fairly unfettered. I pushed her back until she was at arm's length. "Tell me."

"Lola came to me. I was her last hope, her only friend. She wanted out so very much. And I . . . and I . . ." She broke into wracking sobs. I let her pull close again. Between the sobs and gasps I could make out, "And I let her down."

When the crying had settled down I said, "I need your help."

"What?" she said. "To do what?"

"I need to get into Levi's place, to see him. He could be getting ready to skip."

She pulled herself loose from me, spun the other way again. Her shoulders twitched once or twice, in hiccup fashion. She turned back to face me, dragged a robe sleeve across her eyes, held one sleeve end with her dainty fingers and dabbed at the inside corners of her eyes.

When she could look at me clearly, she did so without flinching. "Whatever you think of me," she said, "I won't betray my own brother."

"No matter what he is?"

"No matter."

I looked at her, and tried for a smile, though I have no way of knowing what showed. "To tell you the truth," I said, "that's a positive difference between the two of you."

I pulled up in front of Jimmy Bravuro's south Austin home. Joz was dressed and bustled out to the car. She climbed into the passenger seat and started talking, "You know I'm stuck here without a vehicle. Where the hell you been? Playing cribbage at the church, or what?"

Traffic was light all the way to Levi's gothic house. It looked different in the bright sunlight, but not cozier. I circled the area in a couple of passes from both directions. After all last night's action, the city seemed to be breathing a sigh and taking a rest. I could spot no cars staked out around the place.

I parked the car down half a block. The back of Levi's place fronted along a greenbelt, an area too steep for building where trees and scrub bushes filled in the slope. Joz and I stayed low, scurrying across the back of one sprawling lawn until we were in the greenbelt. It was nobody's idea of a park in there. The vegetation had grown together into a mat of spider's webs and thorn bushes. I pushed through in my already damaged suit. Joz followed close behind.

Dark twisted vines formed walls tight enough to make me wish for a machete. It was dark in the shade of the trees close enough to have formed a low canopy. And it felt clammy warm instead of being cool in the dark shadows. Sweat poured down the inside of my shirt. Thorns grabbed and pulled at the threads of my suit.

"You sure we couldn't have just marched through the front door?" Joz said.

It was too late to matter. I veered close to the back of the lawns. We crouched behind Levi's house. I nodded toward it, whispered, "Think you can crack that nut?"

"Piece of cake."

She reached behind her back, pulled out a gun. It was Cassie's. "Why don't you carry this, for luck?"

I slipped it into my inside left pocket of the suit jacket that already hung heavy enough on me after our hike through the woods.

She scampered off from bush to tree to a storage shed. Then she slipped to the back of the house slid along the side. She found what she wanted, popped open a small box, fiddled around inside. It was daylight, and the burglar system might have been off anyway. But it couldn't hurt to check. At least in bright daylight you rarely have to worry about laser beams, motion sensors, any of that crap.

When she was done with the alarm she fiddled with the lock, then went inside a door along the side of the garage. I looked around, saw no one. I took a straighter path across the lawn than the one she had taken. I zipped across and went inside. Two parked cars sat in the garage, one with enough random damage to make me think it had been present at the battle of the previous evening. Joz stood waiting at the door that led inside to the house. She had it cracked and listened. Her head jerked toward the door. She pushed inside. I followed.

We stood in a long hallway, not the regular hallway that led through the house, but a back way in where there were control panels, a washer and dryer, that sort of thing. The stereo system to the house had been mounted against the wall above a desk covered with papers and a phone. We went past it. I reached and popped open the stereo's CD tray. The disc inside was something called a 74 Min. Professional Recordable Compact Disc. Someone had used a magic marker to write "Lola" near the hole. I slipped it into my other suit jacket pocket, but it didn't have enough weight to balance the gun on the other side.

Joz had a pistol out and in each hand as we eased down the hallway. We heard no sounds from the rest of the house until Joz opened the door at the far end of the corridor. Then we heard a scream. "That sounds like Cassie," I said.

Joz took off in a run down the hallway.

"I do not believe in using women in combat, because females are too fierce."

—Margaret Mead

CHAPTER TWENTY

I made no sound running down the hallway. I could hear the sound of Joz's steps as she ran. At the far end of the hall, the fellow Eva had called Ebbie leaned his head and shoulders around a corner to look down the hall our way. He had a white bandage wrapped at an angle down across one eye. He wore the same black suit. His hand reached up inside his jacket. Joz had both guns raised as she ran. A scream came from the room to my left. I spun and rushed inside the library.

It was Cassie's scream. I knew that for sure now. She hung stretched naked against the bookshelves, her arms and legs extended by the ropes that bound her to the ladder and the corner of the shelves. All her pale skin made a stark contrast to the dark leather spines of books. Her white soft-skinned back was to the room, long blond hair hanging down. Lila had a riding crop pulled back for another blow. Levi rested on his knees by the fireplace. He had stacked the bricks that had lined the bottom of the fireplace one side. He reached inside the hole. Piles of bills bound in bundles stood next to an open bag and a pillowcase that bulged. It looked like Levi planned to make a final withdrawal.

Red lines crisscrossed Cassie's soft rounded buttocks and lower back. Her limbs were stretched as far apart as they could get. It didn't look comfortable. Lila started forward with her next swing. In all the noise of Cassie's screams she had not heard our entrance.

I ran across the room, dove at Lila. My shoulder hit her in the middle of her waist from the side. I heard a puff of air slam out of her, and she doubled like a jackknife as we both tumbled forward into the globe, knocking it off its stand. I stood and whirled. Lila lay there trying to learn how to breathe. Levi rose from his knees. I stepped around one jagged and pointed end of the broken globe stand and started toward him.

He reached to the fireplace mantel and his hand came back down holding a dueling pistol. Levi pointed it at me. I stopped.

"Over here," he said, pointed to the corner to his left, on the other side of the fireplace. He kept the gun locked on me as we passed. He went over to where Lila lay, some of the color just coming back to her face. The cape he wore fluttered behind him.

"Don't you know you shouldn't wear a cape during months that have no 'R'?" I said.

"Shut up," he said. "You cannot rattle me, so just shut the fuck up."

Levi bent to one knee beside Lila. He kept the gun pointed at me.

"I hadn't thought of that," I said. "You had a thing for Lola all those years, but she didn't reciprocate. This doppelganger business may have started out as a way to get her back into whatever cult web you were weaving, but you found you had someone who is a ringer for Lola, and who would let you do whatever you want. Was it like having your cake and getting to eat it too?"

"I said to shut the fuck up." Levi's eyes glittered with all their intensity, and the gun barrel didn't waver. His rich young man's dignity was off-center, though. "And stay put."

I had slid a half step closer toward where Cassie hung naked from the wall. The piles of money and bricks removed from the bottom of the fireplace were an obstacle. It seemed like a lot of money, a couple or three million or more. I was surprised he had let Lila have her moment of recreation when they could have been focusing on this much loot.

Lila sat up, her back against the shelves. Her eyes opened, though they seemed a little crossed to me. I'd hit her a pretty good flying tackle. I doubted if she had played any football in high school.

Joz appeared in the doorway. Her eyes locked on the piles of money, then she forced them away to fix on Levi. "Drop the gun, Batman," she said. She held a gun in each hand. "You're out-trumped."

The barrel of Levi's gun swung until it aimed at Cassie's head. "See you and raise," he said. He rose to tower beside Lila. He couldn't miss Cassie from where he stood. "You put them down on the floor, slowly."

I wasn't sure myself what Joz would do, how much she cared about her sister. There was a lot of money in the room. She bent and put both guns on the carpet. I knew she had a knife and maybe another gun on her somewhere, but all Levi had to do was squeeze his trigger.

I slid another step closer to Cassie, but knocked over a pile of the money. The fallen pile of bundles sprawled in my way.

"I told you to stay put," Levi snapped. Nothing had diminished his being a dangerous man. Joz stood in place, but wound tight, like a cat ready to spring. The two of them in the same room added quite a lot of tension. I slid another half step that knocked over another pile of money.

"You know," Levi said conversationally, "there's a silver bullet in this gun. Pretty classy way to die, don't you think?" He swung the barrel away from Cassie and pointed it at me. He took a couple of steps my way. It was what I had been waiting for.

I leaped over the bricks and money and ran directly at him. The odds were not too good for me, but I knew he had one shot, and that it would take seconds for Joz to have both guns back in her hands.

I sensed rather than actually saw a flash though I didn't miss the loud roar in my ears. Something slammed into my chest like the front end of a skidding Ford. My chest jerked to the left, but I stayed on my feet and ran forward, leaped high and landed on Levi.

He dropped the empty gun and his arms went up to grab me. His knees buckled as my weight in flight hit him high. The two of us toppled, him falling backward. I went into a blur of a tangled roll that ended against the bookshelves, one flailing leg knocking the wind out of Lila again.

I scrambled to my feet and whirled. Joz had her guns, but they hung in her hands at her sides. My eyes swung to where she stared. The black-clad length of Levi lay sprawled in a backward arch over the broken globe stand. The sharp stake stuck up from his chest, bloody. His eyes had frozen open, intense, but shocked and staring in death, and more than a little surprised.

"He shot you, Trav. Right in the chest with a silver bullet," Joz said.

"That only works with werewolves, I think." My chest throbbed, but I was able to move.

I stepped around him to go over and untie Cassie. Lila tried to struggle to her feet. Joz went over and pushed her back to the carpet with one boot.

Cassie collapsed off the shelves into my arms. I took off my jacket and wrapped it around her. It hung heavy on her. I reached to the left inside pocket, took out Cassie's gun. A bullet had smashed into a silver lump against the side just above the trigger guard. It had ruined the gun, but had saved my life. I slipped the damaged gun back into the pocket to leave no trace of us, then put my arms around Cassie to hold her upright.

"You guys were right," I said. "Carrying a gun does pay."

Cassie's initial weakness after being cut down was passing. She spotted Lila and jerked from me and rushed toward her. The jacket fell away. I wished that Levi's cape hadn't been ruined in the fracas. It might have covered her better.

Joz, with both guns tucked away, kept one foot on Lila's chest and pushed the charging Cassie back with both hands. I went over and wrapped the jacket back around Cassie and pulled her away.

"The money," Joz said. "We don't have much time."

True enough. Levi had been scrambling to take his cash and leave. Cassie turned and started to finish the job of getting the bundles of bills into the bag and pillowcases. I looked around until I found the pile of Cassie's clothes thrown behind the bar in the next room.

Joz used the lashings that had held Cassie to tie Lila's wrists to the bookshelves, her back to the books. Her arms were stretched wide. It didn't keep her mouth from going. She muttered a steady low string of curses. Hard to tell who they were directed at, but she stared at the fallen body of Levi where it stretched in an ungraceful arc over what was left of the globe stand. The blood on the stake sticking out of Levi's chest had started to dry.

"Give me your keys," Joz said to me. I was having nothing to do with the money. When I didn't respond, she went over to Cassie and took the keys out of my jacket pocket. She picked up the bag and a couple of the stuffed pillowcases and went out the door.

Cassie had finished packing the money. She stood, shrugged out of my jacket and began to get dressed, ignoring me. She winced a couple of times when the clothing rubbed against the sore stripes on her back. The look she gave Lila, longing to hold her over a flame broil, encouraged me to move over and stand between them.

"I was supposed to be a hostage," Cassie said in a near snarl. "Then the late vampire-boy there agreed to let that woman take out some frustration on me. I expected to be killed when they left."

Joz came back in the room. "It's one long damn hike to that car. Come on, let's go."

She grabbed the last two bags of money and carried them out of the room. I moved toward the door, took my eyes off Cassie for a moment. I heard movement, spun to see her rush to Lila, who thrashed back and forth on the wall. Cassie was swinging as she ran. Her right fist caught Lila in the stomach, hard as Cassie could swing. Lila's legs shot straight out, and she made an "umph." Cassie loaded up and swung with her left and caught Lila on the chin. The blow snapped Lila's head to the left.

I ran back to Cassie and grabbed her around the shoulders and pulled her away. She cradled her left hand in her right. "Oh, oh, oh," she said. "Damn. First thing they tell you is never hit to the skull. It's harder than your hands."

I kept my arms wrapped around her, not trusting that she wouldn't kick the hanging woman or something.

"This is a lovely scene we've got here." The scratchy low voice came from the doorway. Borster stood looking in at us. His gun was drawn, the hammer back. He leveled the barrel at the two of us. He looked at Levi's bloody sprawl and Lila hanging unconscious from the shelves. Then his eyes swung and fixed on the empty hole in what had been the bottom of the fireplace.

He came forward into the room; his gun never wavered and the barrel got closer with each step. I let go of Cassie and moved to arm's length so he couldn't get us both with one shot. "Where's the money?" he said.

I looked at Cassie. She looked at me. From the doorway came another voice, "What we have here is a situation."

It was Joz. Both her guns were leveled at Borster's back. "One a them Mexican stand-offs you hear about."

"Findlay is behind you," Borster said, without turning to look at her.

"And he's horizontal too," Joz said. "You think I wouldn't spot him?"

"Why don't you get over beside your friends?" Borster had still not turned to look at her.

"I like it here behind you." She stepped over to the wall so her back was no longer to the door. "But just so you know, we ain't got a lot of time for chattin' or decision makin', there're cars pullin' up out there."

"Colleagues of mine?"

"Some of them."

"The money," Borster snapped again at me.

"There's a couple of detectives . . ."

"Barnett and Kilgallon probably," I said.

"With half a dozen uniforms for backup. But they're all tied up arguing with a team of INS folks. Quite a tangle out there on the lawn. I 'spect they'll work it out any second."

Borster's lips parted, and he breathed through clenched teeth. It seemed to me that the finger on his gun's trigger tensed and got whiter. "There's only one way out of this," he said to me, "for all of us."

We all had a quiet moment. Cassie broke the silence, "Which is where you get the money, right?"

Borster said nothing. He didn't need to.

"What's on the plate for us?" Joz said.

"You get to live." His voice was the sound a tree limb makes scratching against a glass window on a stormy night.

"Not enough," Joz said. "Travis here is on the lam, and I've always been shy. We need out, and out clean. You've been breathing down Travis' neck too. That ends."

Borster's expression never changed. I watched his shoulders relax and the gun lower a couple of inches. He half turned to look at Joz. He held his left hand out, palm up.

Joz sighed, tucked one of her guns into her belt and dug my keys out of her jeans pocket. She looked at them, then tossed the set to Borster. He caught them in the air.

"Hey, Trav, is that heap insured?" Joz said.

"Of course."

She looked at Borster. "You know what to do then."

He lowered his gun to his side, and with the keys clenched in his other fist he left the room without looking at any of us.

"Now come on," Joz said.

I was slipping on my suit jacket when I saw Lila stir. Her eyes fluttered open. Cassie wheeled and started toward her again. I stepped between them, grabbed Cassie by the shoulders. She tried to squirm past, even raised a knee I caught on my thigh by twisting in time. "Get her out of here," I snapped at Joz.

Joz grabbed Cassie by the upper arm, and though she was smaller, she hauled Cassie out of the room with less effort than it would have taken me.

"I'll catch up," I called to them. I went over to lift Lila's head, lean close and whisper in her ear.

I left her nodding to herself. In the corridor that led to the back, I stopped at the small desk beside the stereo controls, where I had seen a phone and, of all things, a day planner. I lingered there for a few moments, then had to dash out the back and sprint across the lawn.

Cassie and Joz had slipped out of sight in the brush. I plunged into the thick of the greenbelt as a pair of uniformed cops came around to the back of the house and covered the doors. Their focus was on the house. I could hear the cops breaking in the front door as I disappeared into the shadows of the woods.

"What the hell took you so long?" Joz said.

"Hope you didn't stay behind to feel up that tied woman," Cassie said.

Joz let go of a thorny limb she held off to the side of the path. It snapped back and caught Cassie on the front of her thighs.

"Ouch."

"Let's keep ourselves moving," Joz said. "Though we could move quicker if we had the car, and the money."

"That must have stung," I said to Joz.

"You'll never know how much."

Just because a dog lifts his leg at you doesn't mean he's trying to kick you.

CHAPTER TWENTY-ONE

"Don't go the same way we got to the back of the house," I told Joz when she started through the woods. The afternoon air had gotten humid. The greenery was full of thorns. The shadows were not cooling in the dense growth.

"Why not?"

"Chances are, if they follow procedure, that they'll use copters and dogs to comb this greenbelt."

"Better listen to the scout," Cassie said.

"Boy, I'm really glad I gave the car away now." Joz veered to her right and we plowed down the slope through yet unchallenged briars.

"All this may be a little academic," Cassie said, "if that woman starts to flap her gums." A berry branch grabbed at her jeans. She peeled it slowly off the denim and her leg, but never complained.

"We'll see," I said. "If we can get to a phone we might get out before they think to close down the area. No one saw us head this way."

"You gonna just call a cab?" Joz turned her head to glance back at me.

"Something like that."

"Thanks again for the rescue, guys," Cassie said. "But it doesn't look like you planned any of this out very well."

"Why don't you go first for a while, Tonto?" Joz said. "Your suit's pretty well ready for Salvation Army anyway."

"It's the only suit I have," I said, but moved to the lead. There were rips across the pant legs and sleeves, not to mention the hole where Levi's bullet had gone through. My chest still throbbed, busy building a bruise while we hiked. I reached up to make sure the CD I'd snagged was still in my jacket pocket. It was.

The woods began to thin after another fifty yards. We heard no barking police dogs or helicopter sounds.

"You think they're comfortable with the story they're putting together up there?" Joz asked.

Ahead, a row of condominiums to the left wrapped in an arc around a swimming pool. To the right stood some sort of corporate office building.

"What say we B & E a condo and borrow the phone, if that's what you want?" Joz said.

"Why don't I stick my head into the corporate center first and see if there's a pay phone?"

"You see, Trav," Joz said. "That's just why you're no fun in a thing like this."

I glanced at Cassie. She looked away from me.

Making the call wasn't that hard. I found a pay phone down in the basement of the corporate center next to a Xerox machine and a Federal Express pickup box. I made my call and headed back outside, pausing only once when a secretary looked up and down at my suit. "Traffic accident," I said. I watched the paradigm shift on her face change from cautious loathing to pity, but not sympathy.

I slipped back into the edge of the woods where Joz and Cassie sat in a shadow waiting. Cassie swept a spider's web off her shoulder. Her shirt had soaked through with sweat. I had seen the stripes of her lashing marks soak through in pink on the back. Now I looked away from what I could see from the front.

"Jimmy's car will swing through in fifteen or twenty minutes,"

I said. "We'll make a dash for the front of the corporate center then."

"We're sorry about Jimmy," Cassie said. "We know he's your friend, and he pressed us to be able to tell you we were staying there. But you were kind of stiffing us about letting us help anyway by then, and you were never home."

"My place was getting like Grand Central Station." I looked down at the front pocket of my jacket. It hung halfway off. I lifted it, but it fell back down when I let go. "I called Cuthers too, trying to find if you went back there. Just so you don't get it from him, I asked about a boyfriend."

"Oh."

No one said anything for another five minutes. Joz picked up a twig and began to whittle at it, aggressively, as if it was Borster's neck.

Cassie kicked at a loose pile of leaves with her boot. "I thought I was taking the kindest path."

I said, "Sometimes that's telling the truth."

She looked away from me, bounced where she sat and rocked her back into the tree trunk behind her. "Damn." She winced.

"Aw, what the hell," I said. "I'm seeing things more clearly in the playback. I know why you handled it the way you did."

"It's still my fault," she snapped. "You can't steal that from me." Her eyes squinted like Joz's.

I said, "I have a fair idea of what kind of bargain I am. Other than a ready smile and occasional tequila breath there isn't too much to me when I'm not doing my job."

"But you believe in that," Cassie sighed, "and are truly passionate about it. That's to be envied. Truth is, the persistence and the intensity of your morality have always intimidated me, still do, always will. Oh, don't look at me that way. It's hard enough to admit. I found it attractive for a while, but couldn't be around it full-time any more than I could wear ashes and

257

sackcloth. You know," she looked up at me with those pale blue eyes, "maybe I ought to quit the department." She didn't look Joz's way.

"What's that have to do with the way you handled dumping me?"

"It has to do with the way I handle everything."

I kept an eye on the entrance to the parking lot, which I could just see over the crest of a sumac bush. "Maybe you should stay and hope Cuthers can keep working on the 'peace officer' side of you. It might help get the focus off money."

"It won't help me," Joz said. "It was the only way to get Borster off your back for good, and give us an out. But it stings."

Cassie thought for a few minutes more, then looked up with the beginning of a smile. "I did help wrap up the vampire part. It was Levi, wasn't it?"

Jimmy's car pulled into the lot and started for the front of the building.

"Not a moment too soon," Joz said.

"Come on," I said. "Time to move it."

They rose and the three of us jogged out into the open, half expecting police whistles and bullhorns. Instead it turned out to be an easy trot across the grass, tired as we were.

"Wasn't it?" Cassie pressed again as she ran beside me.

I looked ahead to the car like it was the finish line of the New York Marathon. "Come on," I puffed out. "You're a better cop than that. You know we don't have enough on him to confirm anything, much less get an indictment. That's why we were running instead of staying. Besides, I don't think this case is about vampires at all."

Jimmy grinned far too much as the three of us hauled our sour moods into the car. "Where to?" he chirped.

"Just get moving," I said. He pulled out and headed toward

his place, ignored us glancing around in a paranoid watch for patrol cars.

"What now?" I said to Cassie.

Joz answered. It came as a low mutter against the glass of her window. "Guess it's back to the drawing board."

"What happened to the haul you made in that paramilitary mess before this?" I asked.

"You can never have enough for the odd rainy day," she said.

"There had to be over a million there," I said. "I don't understand what drives you or anyone with money to get more, more, more."

"I guess you just don't know what it's like to grow up poor," Joz said.

"Poor?" Jimmy said. I could tell from his tone that his button had been pushed.

"Aw," I said. "Don't get him started." I was too late.

Jimmy smiled into the rearview mirror at Cassie. "He was so poor his momma had to cut the bottoms out of his pockets so he'd have something to play with."

"Quit it, Jimmy." I kept my eyes on the road.

"He was so poor she had to feed him beans if he wanted a bubble bath."

"Stop," I said, louder this time.

He stayed quiet for the next mile, then said, "I was just trying to cheer you up."

"Some other time," I said. The car stayed quiet the rest of the way until we got to Jimmy's house.

Joz and Cassie got out of the backseat and headed for the tent in the backyard. I sat in the passenger seat like a sack of sand, said, "Looks like you might be losing your houseguests."

"Backyard guests. But, yeah, the girlfriend will be glad. Hey, man, I'm sorry about not saying anything about them camping here."

"No need to go into it," I said. "That Joz is gonna give me bad dreams for another year."

Jimmy looked over my suit, the bandage on my face. "Man, you look like the last chapter of *What's the Use?* You been sleeping with a tiger in those clothes, or what?"

"When I started this case," I said, "all I had going for me was a new suit and a new car. Both were gifts, but they were what had made Borster think I had scored well on the last case."

"You never much cared for that car. Admit it."

"No. I didn't. But it went from here to there, without wearing out any shoe leather."

"Hell, a man of your advancing years could stand some exercise."

When I closed my eyes I could hear the low muted sound of a cornet playing some sad and melodious riff. I must have hummed along.

"One thing I like about you, Trav, is that you really do care about music."

"I'm glad you didn't say I have soul, not after all this 'sell your soul to the devil' for success stuff."

He cleared his throat. "As much as I'd like to sit here in the driveway and chat all afternoon," he said, "I've promised I'd go hear Jonesy cut the current CD."

"Maybe I'll see you later," I said.

"That's a new look for you," Vito said, when I showed up at the morgue in a t-shirt and jeans, both borrowed from Jimmy. The t-shirt had FREE TIBET across it in block letters. In a playful mood, Jimmy had scrawled below that, HALF-PRICED CHINA. "Did you bring any more smokes?" Vito grinned. "I'm about out."

"You're a cheery squirrel today," I said.

"I ought to be." He was being mysterious. He waved me

toward his office. We went in and sat at our usual spots. He reached into a desk drawer, came out with two airplane-sized ounce-and-a-half bottles of tequila. He handed one to me. "Only fair to share vices," he said.

"What is it that has you ready to do cartwheels?" I asked.

He poured half his bottle into a paper cup, took a sip from it. He held out another paper cup to me, then saw that I had already emptied my sample.

Vito still grinned—no jutting jaw today. He said, "I don't know how much you know about what's going on. Any idea about what went down at the Damocles' residence today?"

"You tell me," I said.

He took another small sip, shared another grin. "So the cops bust in, find this Damocles guy with a stake through his chest. They don't even put a call out on the air, figuring the media would be down their necks. Your close and personal friend Borster had barely gotten there. He and Findlay arrived there just in time to see a green Chevy Z-71 pickup truck full of men peel out from the house, but too late to save this Damocles guy. His death is no vampire gig, they say—probably happened in some kind of scuffle. Though he may well be our vampire perp, or at least the instigator. An APB's out on the truck. But nothing has come of that. Anyway, they cut down the victim, some woman tied to the wall. Jacobus and those other INS bloodhounds are trying to interview her the whole time. All she can or will say is the name Jake Hunger. She's like a broken record on that."

"Wonder where she got that?" I said. What I had also whispered into her ear was that if she didn't go with that version I was going to personally help the blond lady and her sister find her.

"So check this out." Vito seemed giddy as a schoolgirl. It couldn't have been the tequila. "They run the standard search on the crime scene. They check the phone's auto-dial system, what number do you think they get?"

"Surprise me."

"Jake Hunger's unlisted number. And they find his name, address and number in the address section of a day planner. They gotta run a handwriting analysis on that, think it may not match other entries. But who would write someone else's information in a book like that? Get the whole thing, though, a vampire with a day planner. It was enough to start INS digging into Jake Hunger's affairs in depth, and whatever they've found so far has been enough to take him into custody. Just wait until tomorrow's papers if you think the news has been zippy so far. Jake's ruined in this town."

"That seems to please you."

He dodged the subject. "And our guys're getting all kinds of coded data that may match some of the early vampire stuff."

"But they're getting nothing on the deaths of Lola, Watt Stoner, and Leroy Hunt, right?"

"On the button. Do you know more about this than you're saying?"

"Jeez Louise, Trav. I thought you'd died or something."

"Good to see you too, Owen."

He sat in his office going through liquor purchase receipts when I entered. His office door in the back hallway had been wide open. The place was open for the daytime drinking crowd, but only a couple of patrons had been at the bar when I came in. The Wurlitzer jukebox on the wall was cranking out Fats Domino getting his thrill on Blueberry Hill.

"Hell," he said. "Have you been keeping track of all this wild shit on the news and in the papers? They're saying it's practically a sure thing some vampire got Lola and some others. You ever run down anything for me on what happened to her like I asked?"

"Yeah, Owen," I said. "I did."

"You solved it." He stood up, his chair falling over behind him. "Tell me," he demanded.

"Go ahead," a voice came from the open doorway behind me. "We're dying to know."

I turned. Barnett and Kilgallon both came in. Something told me, from the looks on their faces, that I had not moved forward on either's Christmas list.

"How are you doing, fellows?"

"You still have that suit you wear on almost every occasion I've ever seen you?" Barnett said.

If they were after particle samples they would have to beat the truck to the landfill.

The garbage truck had picked up Jimmy's trash, including what had been my suit, some time ago. I carried the CD that had been in the pocket with me in a clear case Jimmy had given me.

"I'll be more than happy to share everything I have with you fellows if Owen gets to tag along. Will that clear my slate with you, Owen?"

They all spoke at once.

Kilgallon said, "Don't you try to . . ."

I said, "You take me downtown and I get amnesia like you haven't seen it in a while, and I know you guys are getting the whip-crack to solve this."

Owen reached into his desk drawer and came out with a worn blackjack, right in front of the two detectives. "Just tell me . . ."

"Shut up, all of you," Barnett snapped. The room got quiet.

Barnett took deep breaths, trying for control. His words were low and squeezed when he shared them. "I've been on the force for seventeen years, as of two weeks ago. And I will go on record at this time that I have never seen such a tangled mess in all that time as what's going on in town right now." He stopped, took a couple of slow breaths.

Owen and Kilgallon both stared at him with wide eyes. Barnett seemed to look clear through me. "If you can start, and I mean *start* to make sense of any of this for us, I am prepared to listen to you, and take your head off later if needed."

"I'll ride with Owen," I said, "so I can ride in the front seat."

"You'll both ride with us," Kilgallon said, "and the blackjack stays here."

Owen reluctantly put it back into the drawer, but came around the desk looking ready to tear phone books in half.

We all went out into the pounding sun and climbed into the unmarked police car.

*"Want to try that from the top with a reggae
    backbeat in the mixer?"*
"Nix that. This is solid stuff as it stands."
"Variety. We need some peaks and valleys here."
*"I'm tearing out my heart here. Ain't that enough for
    you guys?"*

CHAPTER TWENTY-TWO

The temperature had climbed to ninety degrees by the time we got to the Limping Duck Recording Studio. Even the Palo Verde tree outside had begun to take on the hue of sand.

We went into the air-conditioning of the empty lobby. The red light was on. I waved the three of them to the other door. I held a finger to my lips, then swung the door open.

Jimmy sat tilted back on his chair in the corner. Rob had on the headset, and Stu hovered over the board with all the sliding pegs. They all looked up in alarm as the four of us poured into the booth. Jimmy's chair dropped back down onto all four legs. On the other side of the soundproofed glass, Jonesy sang into the mike, strummed his guitar, his eyes closed in intensity.

"What the hell?" Rob yanked off his headset. Both Barnett and Kilgallon flashed their tins at him. Jimmy's eyes swung back and forth between Jonesy and me.

"Official police business," Kilgallon said.

I'd never heard anyone other than a TV cop say anything like that before, but now wasn't the time to harp on that. I took the small case out of the manila envelope I carried. "Put in this CD and play track seven," I said.

Stu had turned away from the window. "We're in the middle of a . . ."

"How do you think this place'll check out if we have to push?" Barnett asked Kilgallon. "Fire code, books, everything legitimate?"

"Probably have to close the place down a few weeks to find out," Kilgallon said.

It smelled of patent strong-arm cattle flop. But Stu had been around cops about as much as the average citizen. He looked at them, then at Rob. He shrugged. Rob reached for the CD.

In the middle of Jonesy's singing, his backup music stopped. I could see him open his eyes, stop strumming, and glare at the window, could read his lips saying "What the hell?"

Then the CD came on. Lola's voice gave her name and the date, then started the song,

> Each twist of the ladder finds you down one more
> rung,
> Caught in the echoes of songs yet unsung,
> Long since you were promised a home in the stars
> Dim flickers of light seen through smoke in the bars.

Rob and Stu traded looks, ones which visualized their chances of making it rich off Jonesy's CD going in a swirling counter-clockwise motion down the porcelain throne.

The door to the recording room slammed open. Jonesy burst into the room. "What the hell's this bullshit of . . . ?"

The two detectives swung to him, their badges still in their hands. Jonesy's face ran a whole soap opera of emotions. He landed on an outraged look, yelled at Rob and Stu, "Nothin's changed. What do you . . . ?"

"The intravenous device should still be at his house," I interrupted, "unless he's had the sense to pitch it since Hunt's death, which I doubt." The look that flitted across Jonesy's face said he hadn't.

I said, "Then there will be other forensic evidence. You'll be able to place him with means and opportunity for Lola and Watt Stoner. As for motivation, you're listening to it. Lola had the songs together, was going to get listened to by these guys."

Jonesy's mouth had been hanging open, but he snapped it shut. "That's just so much . . ."

"About this device you mention," Barnett said. "How did he come by it? Did he make it, or what?"

"Levi Damocles made it, used it to stir up vampire suspicions. Lola got it from him, took off with it. She'd been living under some delusion that she had some sort of evil twin named Lila. Levi had been controlling her, the same way he was getting Hispanic illegal aliens to work robberies for him out of fear and cult confusion. But she saw through it. At some point she told Jonesy about it, same as she told Watt Stoner and Leroy Hunt. It's why Jonesy had to finish them off too, particularly if he was going to make off with Lola's songs and claim them as his own."

"Lies. Fucking lies," Jonesy screamed.

Kilgallon and Barnett fixed on Jonesy, didn't see Owen's face mottle pink, then red.

"Not only did he lust after Lola's potential recording break, enough to kill her for the opportunity, but his other killings, all as a cover-up in the vampire style to throw blame away from himself, started the flare-up of a war we've had with the illegal alien camps. He's the one who did the awful things to the school kids' pets and called the media to keep the spotlight on vampires. He's responsible for all the deaths of the two warring illegal alien camps, a war he kept stirring up, all to keep attention away from himself."

"There's not a damned bit of it that . . ." It was as far as Jonesy got. He waved his guitar in one hand, his other hand clenched into a fist. On theatrics alone he was making a case for his innocence, but Owen didn't buy it. Perhaps he had seen more of Lola and the changes in her near the end. He leaped between the detectives, knocking them aside, and had Jonesy's throat in his hands. Jonesy dropped the guitar he held.

The detectives stood back for a moment, watched Owen

shake Jonesy's head like a maraca. Jonesy's face progressed from outraged red to near purple. His eyes looked ready to pop. His voice came out as tiny as a penny whistle. "I'll talk. Get him off me."

It was hard to read the expression on Kilgallon's face. But I could make out disappointment on Barnett's. He leaned close to me, whispered, "It's not enough. You want me, and a jury, to buy that he killed three people just to get Lola's songs and a chance at a recording in a studio like this?"

"Hey, ease up," Kilgallon said. He tapped Owen on the shoulder. Jonesy was turning colors I had not seen before. When Owen let up a little, Jonesy grabbed at big jagged gulps of air.

"I wouldn't worry about the coercion rap," I told Barnett. "You're probably gonna deal with an insanity plea anyway. Look." I pulled the yearbook out of the envelope I held, opened it to a page I'd marked near the back. "See, I missed this earlier because his picture wasn't with the other kids. Not everyone is always in a yearbook. But there is this picture near the back."

In the photo I pointed to, Levi Damocles and Darrell Jonesy stood with their arms around each other's shoulders. Both were dressed in dark clothes. Some clever yearbook editor had added the caption beneath them, "Fame and Fortune: Which?" The two of them had been voted most likely to succeed. The caption didn't say at what.

"You check any survivors of the cult," I said, "and I think you'll find Darrell here has ties that go all the way back to the beginning with the others. Ask him now if you like."

"Hey," Barnett said to Owen. "Let go of him."

Owen had been tightening his grip again. Jonesy's eyes had begun to bulge. Owen loosened his grip, let Jonesy's head fall back to the floor with a thud. He lay there gasping like a fish out of water.

We had been talking loud enough for him to hear. Barnett

said, "What about it?"

"An accident," Jonesy wheezed. "Lola. The others . . . things kind of snowballed on me . . . but Lola . . . I didn't mean to . . . we argued . . . then . . ."

Owen lunged at Jonesy again. Barnett and Kilgallon stepped forward. Each yanked on Owen's arms, finally pulled them away from Jonesy's throat. They had to wrestle the still lunging Owen to the other side of the small and crowded room.

Jonesy fell back gasping. "I said I'd talk. I'll tell everything, whatever you want." He put his hands up to his throat. "My voice," he squawked.

"I wouldn't let that worry you overmuch," Jimmy said. "It was never really your strong suit anyway." It was the first harsh thing I had heard Jimmy say.

In the background, Lola's voice filled the booth with another of her songs, one Jonesy had also passed off as his own.

> *What I thought I needed, I let go.*
> *Oh, how I miss it all somehow.*
> *Can't recover, can't beg out,*
> *The devil has it now.*

Cinco de Mayo was coming up, quite a few weeks having peeled by, when Jimmy Bravuro came into my office one afternoon. I had just come in after a thirty-six-hour stakeout of a store where the employees, in some holiday spirit or other, had been ripping off the owner. I labored now with the wrap-up paperwork.

"Hope you don't mind me buggin' by your place, Trav," he said while closing the door. He turned my way. "You look a touch tired."

"Tired? I feel like I had been dragged behind a bus for a dozen blocks. No, I don't mind," I said. "It's good to see a friend."

"You've sure had your share of friends who let you down;

one or two who betrayed you."

"Let me dwell on the ones who haven't pulled out the rug. What's on your mind?"

Jimmy struggled and failed to wrestle back a grin. He put a small gift-wrapped square with a bow onto my desk. "It's Cinco de Mayo out there, in case you haven't noticed."

My office on Brazos Street is too far from the main hum of the city for me to hear the sounds of the festival.

"The holidays come and go," I said.

"You're looking sharp. New suit?" He plopped onto the corner of the desk.

"New to me."

"Open it up." He nodded to the package.

"I didn't get you anything," I said.

"Well, if it's a bottle of blue agave tequila you have in mind, like last Christmas, keep it for yourself."

I unwrapped the gift, a CD in its clear box. A picture of Lola Pillaccherosi was on the front. "You know I don't have anything to play it on."

"New car doesn't have a player?"

"That's a ten-year-old machine. And no, it doesn't."

"Kept some of the insurance money back, eh? You came out pretty well on that deal. You don't have Borster hanging around bugging you anymore. Guess they found the cinders of what was left of your car in Los Angeles. You think Borster went Hollywood on us?"

"No."

"And Joz Brosche is faraway from town, and not likely to visit again soon."

"Yes. But the same goes for Cassie."

"Borster being gone makes up for it, doesn't it?"

I said, "I guess we finally found Borster's price."

Jimmy said, "A lot of us would be willing to sell out if we

only knew someone willing enough to buy."

I didn't say anything, instead looked down at Lola's picture.

"That is, except *you*, man. I never knew anyone as bullheaded as you about doing things the way you think is right, no matter what the cost. You're as rare as a man attracted to women his own age."

"That another little twist of the knife?" I looked up at him.

He surprised me. "Were you ever married?"

"No," I said, "but I was the semifinalist a couple of times."

A soft rap sounded at the door. Jimmy went to open it. I swept up the papers in front of me and was putting them in a file when I looked up and saw a nun. I thought it was Sister Consuela until I saw Eva's face framed in the black and white. She was slim. She was beautiful. She was a nun.

My mouth opened, then closed again. "Wow," I said, when I had my breath back. "That was fast."

"I'm only a novitiate," she said. "I won't be a nun for quite a while."

It seemed hard to picture her a novice at anything. Her smile still showed more Mona Lisa than the Madonna.

"When the police questioned me about Levi," she said, "I never said anything about you heading over there. I got some consolation later out of learning he may have worked his voodoo on illegal aliens, but that he had nothing to do with the deaths of Lola, Watt, Leroy Hunt, or those children's pets."

I searched her face for any sign of hostility, was puzzled at some inner peace instead. She had the exact same enigmatic smile as Sister Consuela.

"You saying you think he was innocent?" I said.

"No. He had become more than half the devil he wanted to be. I know about Rocio, Esteban, the others that were mentioned in the news. He'd have only gotten worse until Lola took the device the cops found at Darrell Jonesy's house—just the way you said they would."

"I wasn't looking into the future. I was looking at the past."

"Oh, don't be like that," she said. "I came to thank you."

"For what?"

"Lots of things. You know that Lola's recordings have rocketed to the top of the charts?"

"I was getting to that," Jimmy said.

"And that the church is getting all the proceeds from the sales."

I turned the box over, read the fine print.

"I am learning," Eva said, "that no matter what happens, some good can come of it."

"No more telling the future?"

"I was never all that good at it. I didn't see *this* coming." She looked down, then let those big eyes slide up to me again. "That's all. I just wanted to thank you, forgive you if you crave that. You're a good man, Travis."

Her voice had gone husky. She turned and went to the door, let herself out.

I still didn't hear any of the Cinco de Mayo music when the door was open, but there was some kind of music in my head. Maybe that lonely saxophone.

Jimmy said, "Now if that doesn't make me want to go home and French kiss the toaster."

"You think that's a waste?" She *had* looked very good.

"You don't? Hell, you're not Catholic. You're not even religious as far as I know."

"I don't know, Jimmy. Sometimes things even out. It did seem that the devil was getting more than his share there for a while."

ABOUT THE AUTHOR

Russ Hall lives by a lake in Texas hill country, northwest of Austin.

Prior to spending his time writing, hiking, and fishing, he worked with major publishing firms, ranging from Harper & Row to Simon & Schuster to Pearson.

He has had more than a dozen books published, including a series featuring Esbeth Walters and a previous collection of short stories featuring the Blue-Eyed Indian, which won the Nancy Pickard Mystery Fiction Award.